She had to get away. . . .

Mom and Dad will tell me that I'm trying to run away from my problems, Christina thought. *Maybe they're right. I don't want the press asking me about Star's times. I don't want my friends wondering why Parker and I broke up. And I really don't want racing to ruin my friendship with Melanie.*

When she reached home, Christina turned off the car and pressed her head against the steering wheel. *I need to do what's right for Star and me. I'm going to get us out of here. If I don't, we'll never be ready for the Derby.*

Collect all the books in the Thoroughbred series

Collect all the books in the Ashleigh series

* coming soon

THOROUGHBRED

DISTANCE RUNNER

CREATED BY

JOANNA CAMPBELL

WRITTEN BY

JENNIFER CHU

HarperEntertainment

An Imprint of HarperCollinsPublishers

HarperEntertainment
An Imprint of HarperCollinsPublishers
10 East 53rd Street, New York, NY 10022-5299

This is a work of fiction. The characters, incidents, and dialogues are
products of the author's imagination and are not to be construed
as real. Any resemblance to actual events or persons, living
or dead, is entirely coincidental.

Produced by 17th Street Productions,
an Alloy Online, Inc., company

HarperCollins books are available at special quantity discounts for bulk
purchases for sales promotions, premiums, or fund-raising.
For information please call or write:
Special Markets Department, HarperCollins Publishers Inc.,
10 East 53rd Street, New York, NY 10022-5299.
Telephone: (212) 207-7528. Fax: (212) 207-7222.

ISBN 0-06-106820-9

HarperCollins®, ®, and HarperEntertainment™
are trademarks of HarperCollins Publishers Inc.

Cover art © 2002 by 17th Street Productions,
an Alloy Online, Inc., company

First printing: February 2002

Printed in the United States of America

Visit HarperEntertainment on the World Wide Web at
www.harpercollins.com

❖ 10 9 8 7 6 5 4 3 2

*To Deborah E. for being my coauthor all those years,
to Amanda V. for being a great roommate,
and to Jessica, my favorite sister*

"EASY, STAR," CHRISTINA REESE MURMURED SOOTHINGLY. She wasn't sure if her words were directed more at Wonder's Star or at herself. Since Star had arrived at Keeneland a few days before, Christina had felt constantly on edge. The crowds certainly weren't helping.

Although it was so early that the sun had just begun to color the sky, the day at Keeneland was well under way. Grooms, trainers, and riders were scattered along the grandstands and the edges of the track, preparing for the morning workouts.

Seventeen-year-old Christina wove her way through a sea of spectators as she led Star to the track. The chestnut Thoroughbred pranced ahead, shying when the reporters got too close.

"Do you think Wonder's Star will have enough

energy to compete in the Bluegrass after his effort in the Louisiana Derby?" one man called out. He shoved his tape recorder into Christina's face.

"I'm sorry, but I have no comment at this time," Christina replied. She didn't want to say something that reporters could use for the next day's headline.

"Brad Townsend thinks that the Louisiana Derby was a fluke. He told me that Celtic Mist would have beaten your horse if he hadn't stumbled," another reporter persisted. She pushed the other reporter aside so she could get her tape recorder near Christina. "He says he's looking forward to a rematch in the Bluegrass."

"We'll just have to wait for the race, won't we?" Christina retorted. She patted her horse, trying to ignore the cameras.

"So are you saying that Wonder's Star will win the Bluegrass?" the reporter continued.

"Sorry, folks. Christina won't be giving any interviews today," Ian McLean, the head trainer at White-brook, interrupted. "She has a horse to work."

Christina smiled gratefully at Ian as the group began to scatter. "Thanks for saving me. I was about to say something I might regret," she said.

"Don't worry. It takes years to learn to deal with them," Ian assured her. "Right now your job is to get Star ready for the Bluegrass."

Star snorted in agreement. Christina put her hands around the colt's neck, laughing as Star pushed his nose against her. "You're already ready, aren't you, boy?" she asked fondly.

"Of course he is," Ian said. "Now, you'd better get on the track. Everyone's waiting."

Christina glanced at the track and saw her cousin, Melanie Graham, riding Perfect Image, a three-year-old black filly. Image had recently overcome some obstacles of her own and, like Star, was being prepped for the Triple Crown.

"How was Image this morning?" Christina asked Ian. The filly had been at the top of her game lately and seemed to like the Keeneland track.

"You'll have to ask Mel. Cindy and I were watching Gratis's work, so I didn't catch Image's breeze," Ian replied.

Cindy McLean was Ian's younger daughter. She had been a top jockey at Belmont until a shoulder injury had forced her to retire. However, the young woman was now helping Vince Jones, a leading Kentucky trainer, prepare Gratis for the Triple Crown.

"It seems like every horse I know is prepping for the Triple Crown," Christina mused as Ian helped her mount.

"Yeah, it's going to be pretty crazy," Ian agreed. "I don't know whom to cheer for. Do you think you could arrange a three-way dead heat between Star, Image, and Gratis?"

Christina forced herself to smile. Since Star's Louisiana Derby win, she had been studying the records of all the Triple Crown nominees. It looked as though Image and Gratis would be the horses to beat, but she wasn't looking forward to racing against her friends.

"You okay, Chris?" Ian asked.

Christina nodded. "Yeah. I was just thinking about today's breeze," she lied, not wanting to share her worries with Ian. She settled into the saddle and rode through the track opening, staying close to the outside rail to avoid the galloping horses on the inside. Star tugged at the reins, eager to run.

"I'll let you gallop soon," Christina promised. She tightened her grip on the reins to keep Star in check. "I just need to talk with Mom and Dad first."

Christina's parents, Ashleigh and Mike Reese, were the owners of Whitebrook Farm, one of the top Thoroughbred farms in Kentucky. Star was the product of her parents' prized horses. His dam, Ashleigh's Wonder, had been one of the only fillies to win the Kentucky Derby, and his sire, Jazzman, had been her father's first stakes winner. Many of Wonder's foals had done great things on the track, and Christina and her parents hoped Star would follow in their footsteps.

"So how does Star feel today?" Ashleigh asked. She ran a hand down the colt's side.

"Pretty good. He handled the mob of reporters better than I did," Christina admitted. "Do you think there's any way I could wave a magic wand and make them disappear?"

Ashleigh laughed and patted her daughter's knee. "I wish. Just remember to stay cool when they're shooting questions at you. We don't want a repeat of what happened before the Louisiana Derby."

Christina sighed. The month before, she had made a fool of herself when a woman from the *Racing Reporter* had asked her questions about Star's recovery from a near-fatal illness. Since then, she had tried to stay away from the press. But the closer they came to Derby day, the harder it was to avoid the reporters. "I'll be careful," she promised for the hundredth time. She checked Star as he jigged sideways and shook his head playfully.

"Well, we'd better gallop this fireball before he decides to breeze himself," Ashleigh said with a smile. "Why don't we do three furlongs today?" Ashleigh consulted her clipboard. "Let him out all the way. I want to see how he likes the surface."

"Sounds good," Christina replied. She eased Star

toward the middle of the track and crouched over his withers as he began to jog. Star fought for rein at first, then gradually settled into a more even rhythm.

Christina smiled as she and Star circled the track. Even though she had ridden Star since he was a yearling, she still enjoyed every moment on her horse's back. From the moment Star had been born, she had shared an incredible bond with him. Since then, they had been through so much together, and with the Triple Crown approaching, it looked as though some of their greatest challenges still lay ahead. The thought of the Kentucky Derby stirred butterflies in Christina's stomach. When Star let out a little buck, she tightened her grip on the reins and forced herself to focus.

After two laps at a jog, Christina readied herself for the breeze. Glancing up the track, she could see her father holding his hand in the air.

When he dropped his hand, Christina kneaded her hands along Star's neck. "Come on, Star!" she called. "Let's run!"

Star responded gamely, lengthening his strides and galloping down the stretch. The wind whipped his coppery mane through the air. And even though the fence posts were becoming a white blur, Christina had ridden Star enough to know that he was holding something back. In the Louisiana Derby Star had burst out of the gate and taken the lead from the start. Even better, he had maintained the grueling pace throughout the race. Christina wanted him to run as powerfully and be as eager to get ahead each time she worked him. She sighed with frustration.

Since he'd arrived at Keeneland, Star's workouts had been adequate but not spectacular. The colt would run to his full potential only toward the end of each breeze, finishing with a flourish and picking up speed with each stride. This meant Star's times for the final furlong were incredibly fast. Still, his overall clockings for the workouts were slower than those of the other Bluegrass entrants.

"Let's go, boy! I know you can do this! Just give me a little more," Christina murmured.

Star responded to her voice, but the burst of speed wasn't as great as Christina would have liked. They passed her parents on the rail with Star still accelerating, yet Christina was sure their time would not impress anyone. She leaned down and patted Star's neck. "What's wrong, Star? You should be grabbing the bit the second I give you the reins." Puzzled, Christina rode back to her parents.

"Good job, Chris," Mike praised. He grabbed Star's reins so his daughter could dismount. "I see he's still taking it easy out there."

"I don't know what to do, Dad. He just won't kick in early on."

Mike put a hand on Christina's shoulder. "Don't worry. He's not a sprinter, so he doesn't need all that early speed. This just confirms that he's a closer, despite his Louisiana Derby performance."

"What was his time?" Christina asked. She patted Star's nose and took the reins from her father.

Mike showed her the stopwatch. To cushion her disappointment, he added, "He ran the last furlong in under twelve seconds, and he was speeding up at the end."

"He can do better," Christina insisted. "Do you think he's getting sick again?" When Star had fallen ill at Belmont the previous fall, his first symptom had been an inability to sustain his usual speed on the track.

Ashleigh shook her head. "Dr. Stevens checked on him before we left Whitebrook and gave him a clean bill of health. Your dad's right, Chris. He's just running like a closer."

Christina wanted to argue, but she had a feeling her parents wouldn't listen. They hadn't been in the saddle on the day of the Louisiana Derby. They couldn't understand how much power Star had shown that day, how well he had run with the early lead. She was the only one who knew what that race had been like. If Star ran that fast in all his races, no horse would ever defeat him again.

"Why don't you give Star to Dani and get on Raven?" Ashleigh suggested.

"But Melanie's jockeying her in the Lafayette Stakes today. Shouldn't she be riding?" Christina knew her mother was trying to distract her so she wouldn't worry, but she wanted more time to think about Star.

"Mel's doing some extra work with Image, and I just want Raven to get a quick jog before things get too crazy. You know how jazzed she gets before a race."

Christina looked over at the small black filly fighting her groom's hold. Dani had to turn the filly in tight circles to keep her from rearing. Reluctantly Christina exchanged Star for Raven. "I'll come visit you later," she promised her horse. "There has to be a reason why you aren't giving me everything you've got."

By the time Christina had ridden Raven and two more Whitebrook horses, the sun was blazing over the track. After being confronted by two more reporters as she made her way to the backside, she decided to take the long way to Star's stall. Instead of walking down the crowded barn aisles, she circled the stabling areas. She passed a row of hotwalkers, thinking ahead to the one race she would be riding in that day. Her parents were putting her on a two-year-old named White-brook's Comet. Comet was showing early promise, and her parents were confident he would break his maiden in the five-furlong race.

She was reviewing her strategy for that race when the panicked cries of a horse interrupted her musings. She turned around and saw a dark bay rearing and trying to jerk away from one of the hotwalkers. There was no one else nearby.

Christina approached the panicked horse, her heart pounding in her throat as she ducked between the rails of the metal fence surrounding the hotwalker. She knew it was risky to get so close to a scared horse, but she couldn't let the horse get hurt. "Easy, easy," she said gently. "You're okay. It's going to be all right."

The horse reared up again, almost flipping over as the hotwalker kept turning. Christina had to leap aside to avoid the slicing hooves.

"Don't worry. I'm going to make this scary machine stop." Christina talked to the horse as she inched toward the center pole, where the off switch was located.

The horse whirled around, blocking her path to the switch. Christina could see the whites of the horse's eyes as it tried once again to pull away. It reared again, this time tangling its lead rope in the spokes of the hotwalker. The line was so tight that the horse's front legs hung suspended from the ground.

Without thinking about what she was doing, Christina grabbed the end of the lead rope and tugged firmly. The knot came loose, freeing the horse.

Once the lead rope was clear of the walker, the horse pulled backward, yanking most of the lead from Christina's grasp. Although Christina had spent years working with frightened young horses, she could feel the muscles in her arms straining as the horse tried to pull away. *I can't win a pulling contest,* she thought. *I have to find a distraction.*

While gripping the lead with her right hand so tightly that her knuckles turned white, Christina fished in her back pocket for a carrot. She stretched out her left hand, offering the treat to the horse. "You're all right," she murmured soothingly. She had to speak slowly to keep her voice from shaking. "Everything's fine now." She looked around, hoping that someone would come and help her.

The horse saw the carrot and took a few shuddering steps toward her. Christina stood still, holding the carrot within the horse's reach. After a long moment the horse lowered its head and ate.

Christina breathed a sigh of relief, even though the horse was still jerking its head at every little sound. As she reached for another carrot, she wished her own heart would stop pounding.

Christina had fed the horse four carrots when she saw a couple approaching her. From a distance their faces looked vaguely familiar. She mentally sorted through names of people from the racing industry, trying to place the brown-haired man with glasses and the tall blond woman. Finally, just as the couple entered the enclosure, she remembered their names: Patrick and Amanda Johnston, a young couple from the West Coast who had made a name for themselves by training the previous year's horse of the year, Matter of Time.

"What happened?" Amanda asked as she hurried over to her horse. "Is Callie all right?"

Seeing the sophisticated trainer in a long lilac sundress made Christina conscious of her own appearance. She was wearing breeches with holes above the knee patches, and her reddish brown hair was tied in a messy ponytail. Fortunately, Patrick was dressed more casually, wearing jeans and a T-shirt. "Um, I—I was walking by these hotwalkers when I saw your horse rearing and panicking," Christina stammered. "I tried to calm him down."

"Well, it looks like you succeeded," Patrick said. He smiled as the horse nudged Christina, trying to find another carrot. "I'm Patrick Johnston, and this is my wife, Amanda." He held out his hand.

"Nice to meet you." Christina quickly wiped her hand before shaking Patrick's. "I'm Christina Reese."

"Aren't you the jockey for that Whitebrook horse, Wonder's Star?" Amanda's blue eyes looked Christina over condescendingly as she spoke.

"Yes, I am," Christina said, trying to appear confident. "And who is this beautiful horse?" She stroked the horse soothingly on the neck.

"Calm Before the Storm, Callie for short," Patrick replied. He patted the horse's flank. "He's running in the Lafayette this afternoon." He paused, glancing at his wife. "Are you scheduled to ride in that race, Christina?"

Christina shook her head.

"How are you at handling nervous horses?" Patrick asked.

Christina remembered how difficult Gratis had been the first few times she rode him. "Uh, it depends on the horse," she replied.

"Can you name some of the more high-strung horses that you've ridden?"

"Well, there are some of the two-year-olds at Whitebrook," Christina began. "And there was Gratis—"

"The crazy horse from Tall Oaks?" Patrick interrupted.

"Yeah. He's not so bad once he gets to know you," Christina said.

"If you can handle him, then maybe you're the rider we've been looking for. How would you like to ride Callie in the Lafayette?" Patrick offered. "His regular jockey in California broke his leg yesterday, and we've been trying to find another jockey all morning."

Amanda touched her husband on the shoulder. "But we were going to have Bonnie Stewart try him out," she interrupted.

"I asked Bonnie. She already has a mount for the Lafayette," Patrick replied under his breath. Ignoring his wife's frown, he continued, "Consider it our thanks for keeping him from hurting himself."

Christina hesitated. She had never ridden a horse in a race without exercising it first. But how could she turn down an offer like this? "I'd love to ride him," she said, rubbing Callie's forehead. "What's his running style?"

"He's a sprinter. If you give him even an inch of rein, he'll take off. However, he's shown some great staying power in his races lately. We're thinking of entering him in a distance race at Santa Anita in a couple of weeks to see if he could be a Triple Crown contender." Patrick took Callie's lead from Christina. "Anyway, we should probably get Callie back to the barn. Stop by in half an hour and we'll talk some more." He looked over his shoulder as he led his horse away. "And thanks for your help, Christina."

"You're welcome," Christina replied. She watched the trainers lead their horse away, wondering what she had gotten herself into.

2

"SO I HEARD YOU GOT A MOUNT FOR THE LAFAYETTE,"
Melanie said as she and Christina pulled their duffel
bags out of their car. Just a week earlier, Christina and
her cousin had pooled their race earnings to buy a
used Chevy Blazer. The car had a few scratches in its
red paint and the air-conditioning was weak, but both
girls were thrilled it was theirs.

"Yeah. I'm a little nervous about it, though. I don't
know anything about the horse." Christina crawled
into the back to get her boots. Because neither she nor
Melanie ever had time to clean it out, the car was lit-
tered with fast-food bags and copies of the *Daily Racing Form.*

"But you get to ride for the Johnstons," Melanie
pointed out. "You're so lucky."

Christina shrugged. "Well, Amanda didn't look too happy when her husband asked me to ride."

"What are you two girls gossiping about?" Cindy's voice interrupted their conversation.

"We never gossip," Melanie said, grinning mischievously. Then she put a finger to her lips and whispered, "But if you must know, Christina's riding a horse trained by Amanda and Patrick Johnston in the Lafayette."

"That's great, Chris," Cindy replied. "The Johnstons are among the top trainers on the West Coast. I'm surprised that they're here at Keeneland, though. Who did they bring?"

"Patrick told me that Calm Before the Storm is their only horse here. He wanted to run him in a sprint stakes race, and there weren't any at Santa Anita this week." Christina had been amazed that the trainer could afford to fly a horse across the country for just one race. Her parents usually vanned all their horses to the various tracks and kept them there for the duration of the meet.

Cindy's blue eyes clouded with sadness. "When I was your age, I helped train an amazing horse named Storm's Ransom. He was the fastest sprinter I ever rode."

Storm's Ransom. Christina remembered hearing the story from her mother when Star had been sick. She had wondered why Cindy, who usually didn't lavish much affection on her horses, had taken a special interest in caring for Star. Then Ashleigh had told her about Cindy's bond with Storm's Ransom, who had died of equine infectious anemia, and Christina had understood.

Melanie gave Christina a quizzical look. Christina responded with a quick shake of her head and mouthed, "I'll explain later." Then she grabbed her bag and said, "We'd better get to the jockeys' lounge."

"Yeah, I'm riding in the first race," Melanie added. "Bye, Cindy! I'll race ya, Chris!" With that, she jogged out of the parking lot.

Christina started to follow, but then she looked back at Cindy, who still seemed sad. Hesitantly she put a hand on Cindy's shoulder. "I'm sorry I reminded you about your horse," she apologized.

"Don't worry about it, Chris," Cindy said with a weak smile. "Have fun out there today."

"Thanks, Cindy," Christina replied earnestly. "I'll do my best."

"He's going to want to go straight for the lead, but hold him back. Keep him within striking distance during the first three furlongs, then let him run." Amanda Johnston paused in her list of instructions to give

Christina a leg up. "He should keep the pace up on his own. If you feel him hesitating, start using the whip."

Christina had heard the same words from Patrick when he had given her the green-and-white diamond-patterned silks of Dreamflight Racing Farm, but she nodded politely.

"And congratulations on your win in the last race," Amanda added.

Comet had won his maiden race by almost two lengths. Christina hoped she could do just as well with Callie. "Thanks," she said warily. Amanda was staring at her as if she was waiting for Christina to do or say something wrong.

As she looked around the viewing ring, Christina swallowed nervously. Across the ring, Ashleigh was giving Melanie some last-minute instructions. For a moment Christina wished she were riding Raven instead of a strange horse.

Beneath her, Callie skittered sideways like a cat. His back legs seemed to move independently from his front legs. Christina was used to horses that felt like a coiled spring before a race, but Callie was breathing hard and sweating as if he had already run the race. "Is he always this nervous?" she asked.

"Usually," Amanda replied. "You'll have to distract him during the post parade."

"I'll try," Christina promised. She leaned down to

pat Callie's neck. "I'll give him the best ride I can."

Amanda nodded but remained silent as the pony rider came to lead Christina away.

Christina tightened her grip on Callie's reins. "I'll show your trainer that I'm a good rider," she whispered to the horse. "We're going to do fine."

As Callie trotted to the gate, Christina tried to get a feel for his rhythm. The colt had more up-and-down motion than Star did. "Well, it's a good thing you aren't going to be a dressage horse," Christina mumbled as she posted. Two years earlier, Christina had been a three-day eventer, devoting all her time to dressage, cross-country, and show jumping. Her love for Star had led her to change her focus from eventing to racing.

Callie sidestepped through the post parade, nearly bumping the escort pony several times as they began warming up. Christina had her hands full keeping the colt moving straight. "Save it for the race," she told the nervous colt. She ran a hand down his side, massaging the base of his neck. "There's nothing to worry about."

Keeping her voice steady, Christina talked to her horse until they reached the starting gate. By then, her mouth was completely dry. She licked her parched lips and checked to make sure her goggles fit correctly.

Callie was one of the first to load. He balked uneasily as the attendants approached. Christina had trouble keeping her balance as the colt twisted and bucked. When an attendant tried to grab the bridle, Callie reared. Christina slipped forward on the horse's neck, then bounced back into the saddle.

"I'm going to push him in," one of the attendants yelled.

"No, let me try walking him in myself," Christina said. She didn't want to spook Callie further. Before the attendant could protest, she repositioned herself in the saddle and pushed the colt forward with her legs and hands. "It's all right, Callie," she soothed. Callie snorted nervously, then walked into the gate. The attendants slammed the doors behind him.

Out of the corner of her eye, Christina saw Melanie expertly guide Raven into the sixth slot. She gave her cousin a quick thumbs-up before grabbing a chunk of Callie's black mane in preparation for the start.

Callie was stamping his feet, trying to find a way out of the confining space. Christina kept up a running monologue to calm both the colt and herself. "I know that I've never ridden you, boy, but let's make a deal. You run your hardest and I'll give you a dozen carrots after the race, okay?"

Callie tossed his head. Christina steadied him and exhaled slowly just as the gate crew yelled that the last horse had loaded.

The starting bell rang, and the gates flew open. For

a moment Christina could see the Keeneland track stretched out before her, a dirt ribbon that seemed to extend to the horizon. Then Callie leaped forward, and the dust from the other horses leaving the gate blocked Christina's vision. They were off!

Instinctively Christina edged Callie toward the inner railing. She wanted to save ground around the first turn. Callie didn't respond to Christina's cues, instead trying to grab the bit in his teeth so he could run faster.

"It's all right, Callie. I'll let you run soon." Christina didn't know if Callie could hear her above the thundering hooves, but she kept talking anyway. "Let's just take it easy right now, boy. Nice and easy." She gave a firmer tug with her left rein, and Callie finally obeyed, though he continued to toss his head.

As she fought Callie through the first furlong, Christina couldn't help comparing him with Star. While Star's gallop was perfectly smooth, Callie moved like a rocking horse. But Callie was definitely running with more eagerness than Star had displayed during his works at Keeneland so far. Even though her arms already hurt from holding Callie back, Christina wished Star would run like this.

Callie jerked his head again, this time pulling a bit of rein through Christina's gloved fingers. Christina could almost feel the colt's frustration at her restraint.

She gripped the reins even harder and gritted her teeth, wondering how much energy Callie was wasting. The colt's stride was no longer a fluid rocking motion. Instead, it had begun to jolt her from side to side.

I can't let him keep fighting me, Christina thought. *He'll burn out.*

The announcer's voice rang overhead. "And after the first two furlongs, it's Speed Demon in the lead, followed by Dashing Glory and Raven. Calm Before the Storm is fourth on the rail, and then it's . . ."

Ahead of her, Christina could see the clump of three horses fighting for the lead. It was taking all of her strength to hold Callie back, and if the colt kept resisting her, he wouldn't have any energy left for the stretch run. Without pausing to consider the consequences, Christina relaxed her grip on the reins. Callie rocketed forward, closing the gap between him and the leaders in two strides.

"Good boy!" Christina praised. She aimed the colt for the narrow opening between Raven and Dashing Glory. Callie gamely ran through it.

"Calm Before the Storm takes the lead by a neck as they finish the third furlong! Raven moves up to second, and Speed Demon fades to third. . . ."

Although she and Callie had the lead, Christina began to get nervous. She knew so little about this horse. What if he didn't have enough to hold on? The Johnstons would be furious with her for disobeying their instructions.

Callie continued running strongly as they headed for the stretch. With a quarter mile to go, they opened up a two-length lead. But the colt was beginning to tire. He wasn't leaning forward as much with every stride, and his gallop had less impulsion. "Just a little more to go, Callie. I know you can do it. Come on!" Christina flicked the whip in front of Callie's eyes, letting the colt see it but not hitting him.

As she continued urging Callie forward, Christina didn't dare break her concentration to look back. Given the sound of pounding hooves, the other horses were probably getting closer. But the wire was only a few strides away. Callie could hold on.

"Let's win it!" she yelled, barely able to hear her own voice. Callie seemed to know that he was close to the end, and he gave one last surge. They crossed the finish line in first!

Christina pulled back on the reins, slowing Callie. "That was a perfect race, boy!" She ran a hand down Callie's sweat-soaked neck. Sweat and dust had transformed Callie's coat from red-brown to a dull black. "I couldn't have asked for anything more."

Callie gave a tired nicker as he dropped to an uneven canter and then to a trot. Christina looked up at the results board, waiting for the final numbers to be posted. An escort rider came to lead her off the track.

"Good job," the rider said. "I think the stewards want to speak to you."

Christina almost dropped the reins in surprise. "What happened?"

"The second-place jockey claims you bumped her horse after the second furlong."

"I didn't bump anyone," Christina said, trying to think back through the race. "Who came in second?"

"I think it was Raven."

"Melanie called foul on me?" Christina's raised voice startled Callie, causing the horse to skitter sideways. She took off her dirt-splattered goggles and looked back at the results board. Callie's post position was listed first, followed by Raven's. "But she knows that I would never interfere with her," Christina murmured as Callie continued jogging.

Melanie was speaking with one of the stewards when Christina rode up to them. Quickly dismounting, Christina threw her stirrups over Callie's saddle and gave the colt another pat on the nose.

A sandy-haired steward approached her. His expression was stern as he asked, "Ms. Reese, can you tell me what happened after the second furlong?"

"Um, I let my horse have the reins, and he responded." Christina tried to sound professional. "I don't think I bumped anyone as we took the lead."

"Ms. Graham says you made her horse flinch with your whip."

"I didn't even use my whip until we were in the stretch!" Christina protested. She wished she could just discuss this with Melanie without the steward there.

"So you deny that you impeded her progress in any way."

Christina knew Melanie was listening to their conversation, so she looked her cousin firmly in the eye. "Yes, I absolutely deny that."

"We're reviewing the tapes upstairs, Ms. Reese. We should have a decision in a few minutes." The steward nodded in dismissal, then turned and walked away, leaving Christina and Melanie standing there alone.

"I had to file the protest, Chris," Melanie said. "I wanted to be sure the race was won fairly."

"But I didn't do anything!" Christina's eyes stung with angry tears. "It was a clean race, and you know it!"

"Or maybe you were so eager to win in front of the Johnstons that you were willing to do anything to get ahead."

Christina was too upset to respond to the accusation. Luckily her parents showed up just then.

"You both rode great races," Ashleigh said calmly.

"It's in the hands of the stewards now, so why don't you go weigh in?"

Christina nodded tightly, then walked over to Callie, who was being examined by the Johnstons. She stripped off the saddle and hurried away before Amanda and Patrick could ask her about the inquiry.

Numb with anger, Christina forced herself through the postrace motions. She had just stepped off the scale when Amanda Johnston came up to her. "Let's get down to the winner's circle. The stewards ruled there was no interference," the trainer said. For the first time, Christina noted some excitement and maybe even respect in her blue eyes.

"That's great!" Christina exclaimed, grinning broadly. She couldn't help looking back smugly at Melanie as she followed Amanda to the track.

"You rode Callie well," Amanda said while they walked.

"His speed made me look good," Christina replied modestly. "I'm sorry I let him out a bit early. I just didn't want him to waste his energy fighting me."

"Yeah, we'll have to work on that if he's going to run in the Derby." Amanda stopped abruptly and turned to face Christina. "Do you think you could come to California and help us retrain him?"

Christina's mouth dropped open. Was Amanda offering her a job? Reality quickly set in, though, and she shook her head. "I would love to ride Callie again, but I have school, and Wonder's Star is my number one priority right now."

"What about during your spring break? When's that?" Amanda asked.

"Well, it starts this Wednesday and goes for a week and a half," Christina answered. "But I'm entering Star in the Bluegrass, so I have to train for that." Christina wished things were different. She had enjoyed riding Callie, and training with the Johnstons was an incredible opportunity. Besides, Callie's running style was the opposite of Star's. If she kept riding the bay colt, she might be able to learn something that would help Star.

"You could fly out to California with your horse and enter him in the Santa Anita Derby instead. The purse is the same as the Bluegrass, and the field will be just as competitive," Amanda reasoned. "Besides, I've always thought that horses do better with an occasional change of scenery. That's why we brought Callie to Kentucky."

Christina's mind whirled. If Star had been running perfectly, she wouldn't have even considered the offer. But maybe Star could benefit from going to California. After all, Star's trip to Montana the previous Thanksgiving had played a key part in his return to the racetrack.

"Do you mind if I think about it for a while?"

Christina asked. "I have to talk to my parents."

"Of course. But we're going to fly Callie back on Monday, so if you want to fly Star out there, you'll have to let us know by tomorrow night." Amanda didn't wait for Christina to comment. "Now, let's get down to the winner's circle before Patrick comes looking for us."

3

"GOOD NIGHT, STAR." CHRISTINA DROPPED A KISS ON HER colt's nose as she prepared to leave the track that evening. "I'll see you tomorrow, okay? I hope our workout will be better."

As she tried to think back to the morning breeze, Christina was surprised at how far away it felt. So much had happened since she had led Star off the track at sunrise. "Yeah, Mel and I were still speaking to each other then," she remarked to herself glumly. She had caught up with her cousin at the end of the day's races to tell her that she was riding home with her parents. Melanie had given her a cold, silent look before walking away.

"What do you think, Star? Do you want to go to California? It would give us a chance to get away from

29

all the craziness here. Think about it—fewer reporters, no more Brad Townsend and Celtic Mist, and we could see how the West Coast three-year-olds are doing."

Star lipped her hair.

Christina laughed. "Is that a yes or a no?"

"Ready to go home?" Ashleigh asked as she walked along the row of Whitebrook horses currently stabled at Keeneland. She stopped to pat Star. "It's great that Whitebrook has serious Derby contenders this year," she remarked. "It's been a while since we were a part of this. You were ten, remember?"

"Yeah, Honor and Glory," Christina replied. "But you had a Triple Crown winner before that."

"Now that really was a long time ago," Ashleigh murmured. Then she changed the subject. "Are you and Melanie still fighting about today's race?"

"We'll work it out," Christina said, trying to sound nonchalant. "You don't think I interfered with her and Raven, do you?"

"I think that both you and Melanie really wanted to win this race. Both of you are too competitive for your own good sometimes. But I know you didn't deliberately interfere." Ashleigh sighed and brushed back the strands of brown hair that had come loose from her ponytail. Unlike Amanda Johnston, Ashleigh usually dressed casually at the track, changing into business clothes only on the days of big races. "If you aren't avoiding Mel, though, why didn't you go home with her? Isn't Katie's birthday tonight?"

Katie Garrity was one of Christina's best friends. For her eighteenth birthday, Katie was having an all-girls slumber party. "Yeah. But I wanted to talk with you and Dad first."

"Well, let me finish checking on the horses before we go find your dad." Ashleigh made a note on the chart by Star's stall and fed the colt a piece of apple before moving on to the next horse.

"Wish me luck, Star," Christina whispered. She gave the colt a hug, then hurried down the aisle to help her mother.

Twenty minutes later, Christina sat in the backseat of the truck, half listening as her parents discussed plans for the next day. At last Ashleigh said, "I think Christina wants to tell us something."

Christina leaned over the seat back so that she could see her parents. After taking a deep breath, she summarized the Johnstons' offer.

"I don't think that's a good idea, Chris," Mike said when she had finished. "Moving Star to California when all the Triple Crown races are on the East Coast doesn't make sense."

"But remember how much going to Montana helped Star?" Christina pointed out. She still wasn't completely sure about California herself, but she

31

didn't want her parents to dismiss the idea before she'd had a chance to even think about it.

"Star was coming back from a serious illness then. He doesn't have any problems right now," Ashleigh said. She turned around to look at her daughter. "Besides, I don't like the idea of you taking Star to a trainer I don't know."

"The Johnstons wouldn't be training Star—I would. They just said I could use their facilities," Christina argued. "If you want, you could write out a complete schedule for him. I promise I would follow it."

"We still don't know the Johnstons, though. They came out of nowhere and trained the Horse of the Year last year, but not everyone has good things to say about them," Mike said. "I know Vince Jones doesn't like them."

"Vince Jones doesn't like most trainers," Christina said dismissively. "Maybe a change of scene would help improve Star's times."

"His times have been fine lately. See for yourself." Ashleigh handed her clipboard back to Christina. "He's a little slow at the start, but he's just adjusting to the Keeneland track."

"Star never needs time to adjust. He hasn't been running up to his full potential here. If we don't turn things around soon, he'll have no chance in the Bluegrass or the Derby." Christina shook her head. She could see Star's times were off, so why couldn't her parents? They were so busy giving her excuses for the slow workouts that they weren't helping her solve the problem.

"Didn't I just warn you about being too competitive?" Ashleigh asked, half smiling. "I know you're always worried about Star, Chris. But California isn't the answer. Maybe the Johnstons will bring some more horses to Kentucky and let you ride them then."

"That isn't the point. I need to do this now," Christina insisted. "Star needs—"

"Listen to what you're saying, Chris," Mike interrupted. "Do you really want to take Star to California a little over a month before the Derby? The Triple Crown races are incredibly grueling. Tiring Star out with traveling will only hurt his chances."

Christina wanted to protest, but she had a feeling that she wouldn't be able to change her parents' minds right now. She resolved to think of better arguments.

When Christina got home, Melanie was waiting by the door, wearing a skirt and a halter top. "Katie's party started ten minutes ago. Where have you been?"

Not wanting to fight in front of her parents, Christina replied, "Just give me a sec to get ready." She ran up the stairs and hastily changed. Breathless, she hurried back down the stairs. Melanie was still standing by the door.

"You want to drive?" Melanie asked. Her voice was flat.

"No, you go ahead," Christina replied. She wanted time to think about the Johnstons' offer. Before the race that afternoon, Melanie would have been the first one she talked to about it. But now she couldn't ask for her cousin's opinion.

Christina and Melanie drove to Katie's house in complete silence. Melanie watched the road while Christina stared out the window, wondering if her parents were right about California.

Several cars were already parked in the driveway when they arrived. Christina recognized the red Mustang that belonged to Kaitlin Boyce, the girl who was leasing Christina's event horse, Sterling Dream.

Mrs. Garrity greeted them at the door. "The other girls are in the hot tub," she said.

While Melanie went to change into her swimsuit, Christina went directly to the hot tub. "Happy birthday, Katie!" she called as she stepped onto the back porch, shivering in the cold night air.

"Thanks, Chris!" Katie said. "Why aren't you wearing your swimsuit?"

"It's been a really long day," Christina replied. "I only want to put my feet in." She sat down on the edge, between Barbara and Charlene, two girls who had starred with Katie in the school's production of *Grease* the previous fall.

"Did you win any races today?" Charlene asked.

"Yeah, I had a pretty lucky day," Christina said. She quickly told the others about Callie, not wanting to bore them with too many horse details but needing to share the good news with someone. She deliberately omitted any mention of Melanie.

"You still haven't taken me to the track," Yasmin, another girl from the drama club, said when Christina finished.

"Well, if you all weren't going to Maui for spring break, then you could watch me and Melanie ride at Keeneland," Christina pointed out. The other girls there were spending a week in Charlene's family's condo. She and Melanie had both been invited, but they couldn't leave so close to the Derby.

"I wish you could come with us," Katie said.

"I don't feel too sorry for her. She's going to be famous," Michelle teased. Michelle also rode horses, but she focused on show jumping.

"Yeah, Chris, you have all the luck," Barbara agreed. "You're going to win the Kentucky Derby, plus you have the cutest boyfriend in the world."

Christina tried to smile. She hadn't told anyone except Katie and Melanie about her relationship problems. But between her dedication to racing and his focus on the Olympics, she and Parker Townsend hardly saw each other anymore. A couple of weeks before, she had finally suggested that they take a break from each other.

Visiting Parker during the Rolex competition the previous weekend had almost changed Christina's mind. Parker had ridden a flawless cross-country round and vaulted to first in the standings after the second day. However, he decided to scratch his horse, Foxglove, from stadium jumping after she went into shock from heat exhaustion. When Christina left the show grounds, Parker looked so upset, she wanted to do or say something to help him. But she'd kept her distance, not wanting to make any promises she couldn't keep.

"Before you ask, Chris, Foxy's doing okay," Kaitlin assured her. "The vet checked on her again yesterday."

Christina breathed a sigh of relief.

"So what gossip did I miss?" Melanie ran across the porch and slid into the hot tub between Lindsey and Dominique, two girls from the soccer team.

"Chris was just telling us about her day at the track," Katie answered. "Did you win any races today?"

Melanie glared at Christina. "No, some majorly competitive jockey interfered with me."

Christina clenched her hands into fists. She interrupted Melanie, changing the subject to avoid a confrontation. "But you've all probably had enough horse talk for the night. What are we going to do next, Katie?"

"Oh, typical slumber-party stuff. Watch cheesy movies, paint each other's nails, maybe play Truth or Dare."

"You're turning eighteen, not twelve," Dominique teased.

"I know. I just feel like being silly," Katie replied.

True to Katie's word, the girls spent the rest of the evening playing an increasingly outrageous game of Truth or Dare and then sprawling out in the living room to watch the Indiana Jones trilogy. However, Melanie and Christina had to leave after the first movie so that they could get some sleep before going to the track at dawn the next morning.

Once again they drove home in silence. This time Christina was at the wheel. She had just turned off the main road when she noticed Parker's truck parked at the side of the drive. She stepped on the gas, wondering what he was doing at Whitebrook after midnight.

Parker was standing by the front paddocks, petting one of the mares. He waved at Christina and Melanie when they got out of the car. Melanie waved back before quietly going inside.

Parker walked toward Christina slowly. "I called your house earlier, and your mom said you would be back pretty late," he said hesitantly. "You're probably tired, Chris, but I really wanted to talk to you."

Christina nodded, stifling a yawn. "Yeah, we do need to talk," she agreed. She looked into Parker's intense smoky gray eyes, wondering what he was thinking. A few months before, they had been so close. They would talk to each other for hours without running out of things to say. Now Christina felt as though she didn't know what to say to him.

"First of all, I wanted to tell you the great news," Parker began. His lips tightened into a thin smile. "Mark Donnelly offered me a USET grant to train in England. I just finalized all the details this afternoon."

"That's awesome, Parker. Congratulations!" Getting United States Equestrian Team sponsorship had been one of Parker's dreams, the first step on the path toward the Olympics. Lately he had been stressed that the committee would never notice him and Foxy. Christina wanted to hug Parker, but she held back. Instead, she walked over to an empty turnout and sat on the rail, motioning for him to sit beside her.

Parker didn't move. He stood by the fence, turning to face her. "I'll be leaving for England with Foxy after school gets out. I hope I'll be allowed to bring Ozzie, too." Ozzie was Parker's new horse. The gelding had burned out on the Grand Prix jumping circuit, and his former owner had practically given him away. But Christina was sure that Parker was talented enough to turn any horse around.

"What about school?" Christina asked. Parker had given her a hard time when she had told him she was taking a year off before starting college. Was he going to do the same thing now?

"After Burghley I'll come back and start classes," Parker replied.

Christina's eyes widened. Burghley was a four-star international event. Parker was definitely on his way to making the Olympic team, even though he'd never admit it himself.

"I couldn't sleep the night after Rolex," Parker continued softly. "I kept thinking about Foxy and how close I came to losing her. And then I remembered how you were there for me, despite the fact that I haven't been here for you lately."

"What are friends for?" Christina twisted her hands in her lap as she waited for Parker's response.

"I also kept thinking about the way things have been between us for the past month, especially since we decided to spend some time apart," Parker said. "I guess I just want to know what you think we should do now."

Christina closed her eyes, trying to think. Part of

her wanted to tell Parker that they should get back together and work everything out. However, she knew that neither of them had the time to fix their relationship. Parker needed to prepare for Europe, and she would be busy with Star and the Triple Crown. Her eyes began to fill as she realized what she had to say.

"I'm sorry, Chris. I came at a bad time," Parker apologized, breaking the silence. "I shouldn't have thrown all this on you tonight." He pulled his keys out of his pocket.

"No, Parker. You're right. We need to resolve this." Christina bit her lower lip to keep it from trembling. "And I think we both know what we should do."

Parker played with his keys for several moments before nodding. "We're going to hurt each other if we keep going, aren't we?"

"I think so," Christina whispered. "So maybe we should really end things before it comes to that." She looked at Parker tearfully, unsure which answer she wanted from him.

"Yeah." Parker was blinking back tears, too. "I can't believe this is happening."

"Neither can I." Christina could no longer meet Parker's gaze. "But you'll still keep me up-to-date on what's going on with you and Foxy, right?"

"Of course, as long as you fill me in on all the races

you win with Star." Parker's voice was muffled as he hugged Christina tightly.

Christina rested her head on his shoulder one last time before reluctantly pulling away. "I-I'd better go inside," she stammered. "I have to get to the track tomorrow. Melanie likes to leave early, and . . ."

"I understand." Parker said, already walking toward his truck. "I'll see you later, Chris."

"Bye, Parker," Christina said, stifling a sob. She watched him until he started the engine, then turned around so he couldn't see how upset she was.

For the next half hour Christina wandered through the Whitebrook barns in a daze. "It was the right thing to do," she kept telling herself. "Things weren't working anymore. I knew this was coming."

Mechanically Christina paced from stall to stall, repeating these words to force back the lump in her throat. When she reached the isolation stall at the end of the aisle, though, she remembered how supportive Parker had been when Star was sick. He had kept her spirits up even when everything had looked so hopeless. Tears welled up into her eyes, and she was unable to control her emotions any longer.

Sinking to the ground, Christina put her face in her hands and cried tears of sorrow and exhaustion.

4

"WELL, YOU'RE GOING TO HAVE TO DO ALL THE WORK today, Star." Christina yawned as she took Star's reins the next morning. She had already ridden three other Whitebrook horses, and the lack of sleep was catching up with her.

"Need a leg up?" Mike asked.

"Sure." Christina let her father boost her into the saddle. "Doesn't Mom want to watch?"

"She's checking on Mel and Image," Mike replied. He looked at her critically. "Are you feeling all right? You have huge circles under your eyes."

Christina sat up straighter. "Don't worry, Dad. I'm fine."

"Okay, well, you know the drill. Jog him a couple of

laps, and then we'll do another three-furlong breeze. I'd like to see him a bit sharper today, but don't push too hard."

"I'll do my best." Christina rode Star onto the dirt track. The colt immediately broke into a trot. Christina posted to the gentle, familiar rhythm.

Star snorted as a horse breezed past on the rail. He leaned his head forward, pulling on the reins.

"Hold on a sec, boy. I don't think Dad would appreciate it if we just took off before you warmed up properly." Christina couldn't help smiling, though. Star's eagerness boded well for the upcoming breeze. Perhaps her parents were right. Maybe Star had needed a few days to get used to Keeneland.

After another lap at a jog, Christina watched the markers on the side of the track. She angled Star to the rail, making sure she wasn't cutting any horses off.

Anticipating the run, Star extended his trot, leaning against the bit. "Just a little longer," Christina assured her horse. She waited until the five-eighths pole, then gave Star his head.

Star leaped forward, showing speed Christina hadn't felt since they had been at Fair Grounds in Louisiana. The colt's long strides ate up the dirt. Christina praised him, hoping he would keep up the pace.

But toward the end of the first furlong Star's

impulsion faded. His strides shortened, and Christina had to drive him forward with her hands. "Don't quit on me now," Christina said, gritting her teeth. "Come on, Star!"

Star's ears flicked back at the sound of Christina's voice, but he didn't increase his pace until he had finished the second furlong. Then he pushed forward again, picking up speed with every stride and blurring the world around them.

Christina stood in her stirrups at the end of the breeze, frustrated. What had happened to Star since he won the Louisiana Derby? Why wouldn't he move forward throughout the workout?

"I wish you could tell me what's wrong, Star," Christina said as she trotted him back toward her father. "Is it something I'm doing?"

Mike was looking down at his clipboard when Christina rode up to him. "His time was faster than yesterday's," he said. "Any idea what happened during the second furlong?"

Christina shook her head. "I don't know," she replied. "He's making his own decisions about when to show speed." She sighed. "How can I make him go faster?"

Mike patted his daughter's knee. "I wouldn't worry about it too much. Like your mom said yesterday, he might not like the surface. Besides, I don't want to work him too hard before the Bluegrass."

"But I've checked the times of all the other Bluegrass entrants," Christina protested. "All their fractions are faster than Star's."

"Not by much." Mike glanced at his clipboard again. "If you really think he's not paying attention, though, you could always try carrying a crop during the breezes."

"You know I can't do that, Dad. It might remind him of what happened at Townsend Acres." Christina hugged Star protectively. Star's experiences with Ralph Dunkirk, the harsh head trainer at Townsend Acres, had made him distrustful of people. It had taken months for Star to trust her again.

"Well, it's your choice. Personally, I think Star would be fine either way. He knows you won't hurt him with the crop, but he's running fine without one," Mike said. "Now why don't you go see if your mom or Ian needs you to work any other horses?"

Christina obeyed glumly. She couldn't understand her father's lack of concern. Star could do so much better. If he was going to run in the Triple Crown, he would need to.

Ashleigh was standing farther up the track, talking with Melanie and Ian.

"Why don't we breeze Image four furlongs today?" Ian asked. "She's been burning up the track since we got here."

"Sure, I know she—" Melanie stopped abruptly when she saw Christina.

"Oh, hey, Chris. How did Star do today?" Ashleigh asked.

Christina tried to smile. "The usual," she replied. She didn't want to talk about Star's problems with Melanie there. "Dad seemed satisfied. Anyway, I was just wondering if you wanted me to work some more horses."

"I don't think so. Why don't you go check with Maureen? Or you could just hang around and watch Image breeze."

Melanie opened her mouth, preparing to protest, but Christina shook her head before her cousin could say anything. "I'll go find Maureen," she said.

A relieved look crossed Melanie's face. Christina walked away before her cousin could start glaring at her again.

On her way to see Maureen Mack, Whitebrook's assistant trainer, Christina stopped by Callie's stall. Patrick Johnston was there, checking on the colt.

"Hey, Christina!" he called as he ran his hands down Callie's front legs. "Have you decided to come with us to California?"

"Um, my parents are still thinking about it," Christina answered, hoping he couldn't tell she was lying. "How is Callie doing?"

"He's fine. He was off his feed last night, but he's eating again now," Patrick said.

"When's his next race?" Christina patted the horse's nose.

"Amanda wants to run him in the San Felipe Stakes. It's a mile and a sixteenth, so we'll need to change his running style before then," Patrick said. He handed her a copy of the *Daily Racing Form*. "He ran his fastest yesterday in the fourth and fifth furlongs. We have to make him delay his run in the longer races so he'll have more power at the finish."

Christina checked the times for Callie's race. Star's times from the morning's breeze made Callie's early fractions seem even more impressive.

"We'd love to have you work with him," Patrick said. "He's sort of a picky horse, so once we find someone he likes, we try to stick with that person. Besides, I think yesterday was his best race yet."

Christina blushed. "I'd love to ride Callie again. I'll check with my parents again this afternoon and let you know tonight." She paused, then added, "I'm pretty sure they'll say I can go."

Patrick smiled. "Great. I'll look into getting a ticket for you and Star, then."

As Christina walked away from Callie's stall, she berated herself for lying to Patrick. After her conversation with her parents the day before, she was nearly certain they would never let her take Star to California.

"But I'm going to go crazy if I don't get away from here," Christina murmured as she made her way to the Whitebrook stables. She hardly paid attention to the people passing by until she heard a familiar voice.

"So I hear Wonder's Star had yet another mediocre workout."

Christina looked up to see Brad Townsend striding toward her. Despite the early hour, he was already dressed for the winner's circle, wearing a tailored suit with gold buttons.

She greeted him with forced politeness. "Hello, Mr. Townsend."

"It looks like the Louisiana Derby took all your horse had," Brad continued.

Christina shook her head. "The Louisiana Derby field was good, but Star can handle better," she said carefully.

"Well, you won't get lucky again during the Bluegrass. I've replaced George Valdez with Douglas Aikman. Perhaps you've heard of him."

Christina swallowed. Douglas Aikman had won an Eclipse Award the previous year.

Brad smiled. "Anyway, Celtic Mist seems to love it

here at Keeneland. He's been putting in black-letter workouts left and right."

Christina bit her tongue in an attempt to hold back a retort. Still, her temper got the best of her. "Celtic Mist had some pretty fast workouts at Fair Grounds, too, but as the Louisiana Derby proved, it's what happens on race day that really counts." Before Brad could reply, Christina hurried past him.

After leaving Brad, Christina moved through the backside as quickly as she could, hoping to avoid anyone else she knew. She had almost made it to Star's stall when she passed Cindy, who was talking to a throng of reporters. Cindy waved before Christina could duck away, drawing the reporters' attention to her.

Reluctantly Christina walked over to the group. A reporter hurried over to her. "Cindy was just telling us that Bonnie Stewart will be riding Gratis for the Blue-grass. Why did you choose Wonder's Star over Gratis as your mount in this race?" he asked her.

"Star has been Christina's horse since he was born. Of course she would choose to ride her own colt," Cindy replied for her.

"But the word on the track is that Wonder's Star won't be able to keep up in the Bluegrass. His workouts have been pretty slow lately. Can you confirm that, Christina?"

"Leave her alone," Cindy snapped. "Christina and

I have to go check on a horse." With that, Cindy put an arm around Christina's shoulder, turning her away from the crowd. When they were out of earshot, Cindy whispered, "Sorry to put you through that, Chris. I just called you over as an excuse to escape." She took a breath and blew it out. "You know how much I hate giving interviews."

Christina tried to smile at Cindy's comment, but she couldn't get the reporter's words out of her mind. They had confirmed what she'd been worrying about herself. Star's workouts were not up to par.

"Are you all right, Chris?" Cindy asked, concerned.

Christina nodded distractedly.

"Are you sure you're okay? You look a bit pale," Cindy said. She put a hand on Christina's forehead.

Christina pulled away. "I'm fine," she insisted. "I just didn't get much sleep last night."

"So why don't you go home and rest?"

Normally Christina would have resisted that suggestion. But she didn't feel up to spending the day at Keeneland anymore. She didn't want to be reminded that the big races were coming up and that Star wasn't ready for them. "Maybe I should," Christina replied. "Could you tell Melanie I took the car?"

Cindy looked surprised that Christina had agreed to go home so readily. "Sure. I'll let her know," she said. "Just get some sleep, okay?"

Christina gave Cindy a tight smile. She walked to her car without even saying good-bye to Star. Although she wanted to see her horse, she didn't want to risk bumping into her parents or Melanie and having to explain why she was leaving.

During the drive home, Christina tried to calm herself using the visualization technique her friend Lyssa Hynde had taught her before the Louisiana Derby. She pictured Star winning the Kentucky Derby, crossing the finish line at Churchill Downs ten lengths ahead of his competition. The announcer would be screaming that her colt had just shattered the stakes record, and she would pose for the photo in the winner's circle, promising the crowds that her horse would be running in the Preakness and the Belmont.

But as Christina thought about Star crossing the finish line, she remembered the other horses in the field—Celtic Mist, Gratis, Image. . . .

The thought of Image brought Christina's mind back to reality. She didn't want to think about beating her cousin, especially not after the fallout from the Lafayette.

"Melanie and I used to compete against each other without any problem," Christina thought out loud. "What's the big deal?"

The words had just come out of her mouth when Christina realized the answer to her own question. The nature of her competition with Melanie had changed when both Star and Image became Derby contenders. Christina knew that Melanie loved Image as much as she loved Star. Until now they had managed to keep the two horses' schedules separate. But soon the two of them would meet.

How can I want to win more than anything if it means Image has to lose? Christina wondered. *And what about Cindy? I want her to win with Gratis, too.*

Christina sighed. She had to get away from Keeneland. She knew she couldn't keep the horses from racing against each other forever, but taking Star to Santa Anita would at least delay the inevitable.

Mom and Dad will tell me that I'm trying to run away from my problems, Christina thought. *Maybe they're right. I don't want the press asking me about Star's times. I don't want my friends wondering why Parker and I broke up. And I really don't want racing to ruin my friendship with Melanie.*

When she reached home, Christina turned off the car and pressed her head against the steering wheel. *I need to do what's right for Star and me. I'm going to get us out of here. If I don't, we'll never be ready for the Derby.*

"So, which one of you wants to tell me all the latest track news?" Samantha Nelson, Cindy's older sister, asked at dinner that night.

While everyone else started to speak at once, Christina stared at her half-eaten plate of pasta. Although Beth McLean, Ian's wife, was an excellent cook, Christina had only been able to pick at her food all evening. She had spent the entire afternoon trying to think of ways to convince her parents that she should go to California. She had planned to talk with them the moment they returned from the track, but the first words out of her mother's mouth when she got back from Keeneland were that they were going to the McLeans' cottage for dinner.

"Well, thanks to Cindy, Gratis will be ready," Ben al-Rihani, Gratis's handsome owner, replied. He smiled warmly at Cindy. "Since Rush Street's been having trouble lately, all of Tall Oaks' Triple Crown hopes rest with Gratis now."

"As you can tell, Ben likes to keep the pressure off me," Cindy joked. Christina couldn't remember seeing her friend so relaxed and happy.

"Any other Triple Crown gossip?" Tor, Samantha's husband, wondered. Both Tor and Samantha trained eventers, jumpers, and steeplechasers at Whisperwood Farm.

"Well, a lot could happen in the next few weeks," Mike said. "We'll know who the real contenders are after the Bluegrass and the Santa Anita Derby."

"Who are the big West Coast horses this year?"

Kevin, Samantha's younger brother, asked. Kevin was the same age as Christina and Melanie. He and Melanie had dated for a couple of years, and he had played a big part in Image's early training.

"Supposedly the horse to beat there is a colt named Pocket Money," Melanie said. "He's won his last four races."

Seeing her chance, Christina jumped into the conversation. "Maybe Star and I should go to Santa Anita and give Pocket Money some competition."

"We've already discussed this, Christina," Ashleigh said. She gave her daughter a warning look. "You aren't taking Star to the West Coast."

Now Christina had everyone's attention. Trying to ignore all the stares, including Melanie's pointed glare, she began her rehearsed argument. "I know you've always run your Derby contenders in the Bluegrass, but maybe Star and I shouldn't take the same road to the Kentucky Derby as all the other Whitebrook horses. Maybe it would be better if we got away from the local pre-Derby drama for a while." Christina stopped and took a deep breath.

When no one said anything, she continued. "Star's times have been off lately, and I think it might be my fault. I can't concentrate at Keeneland with Melanie and Cindy and everyone competing against me. If Star and I go to California, I'll have more time for him. You know Star always responds best when I work with him exclusively. The Johnstons say I can keep him at their farm. He'll love the peace and quiet—it would be healthier for him than the tension at Keeneland." Christina realized she was babbling, so she cut to her final argument. "The competition for the Santa Anita Derby will be just as good as the competition in the Bluegrass, and the purse is the same. Dad just said it himself—these two races will really narrow down the field of Derby contenders."

"I still don't want you working with trainers I don't know very well," Ashleigh replied.

"Like I said before, I'll call you every night and tell you what's going on," Christina said. She looked around the table as she spoke, wishing one of the others would help her. Normally Melanie would have come to her defense, but her cousin was avoiding her gaze.

"But we were planning to build Star up for the Triple Crown slowly. The Santa Anita Derby is a week before the Bluegrass," Mike pointed out.

"Star will be ready," Christina said. She clenched her hands into fists under the table, trying not to let frustration creep into her voice. "And if he runs in the Santa Anita Derby, he'll have an extra week to rest before the Kentucky Derby. Please, Mom and Dad, I know going to California is the right thing for me and Star."

"Before you say anything, Ashleigh, think about

the Dubai World Cup, where Limitless Time raced against Champion," Cindy interrupted, causing everyone to look at her. "I'll never forget how hard it was for me to ride against you. I was so excited to be jockeying in that huge race, but for a long time I had trouble concentrating because the idea of competing against you worried me so much."

Ashleigh half smiled. "Yeah, things got a little tense there, didn't they?"

"And Samantha, do you remember the time when we thought Shining and Glory could be racing against each other in the Breeders' Cup Classic?" Cindy asked. "I must have bugged you for weeks, hoping that you would run Shining in the Distaff instead. It took us forever to be honest with each other about things."

Samantha nodded. "It's never easy to compete against family and friends," she agreed.

"So maybe we should be applauding Christina for being honest about how she feels," Cindy said, smiling ruefully. "You should let her go, Ash."

Christina wanted to hug Cindy, but she remained silent, knowing that she would only hurt her chances by speaking now.

"Cindy's right," Samantha said. "Besides, we all know Christina always has Star's best interest at heart. She gave up Sterling so she could focus on the colt."

Ashleigh and Mike exchanged looks. "I think we

should give the Johnstons a call before we decide anything," Ashleigh said carefully.

Christina pulled the Johnstons' business card from her pocket and handed it to her mother. "I'm sure they'll be happy to answer any of your questions," she told them. She crossed her fingers behind her back, hoping that the Johnstons could reassure her parents that Star would be well cared for at Dreamflight, their famously luxurious farm.

After her parents went into the kitchen to use the phone, Christina strained her ears to hear their conversation. She was too excited to eat. She half listened to the small talk going on around her, offering her congratulations as Kevin discussed his soccer scholarship from Kentucky State. Every once in a while she looked across the table at Melanie, wanting to see her cousin's reaction. But Melanie kept playing with her pasta, ignoring Christina.

Finally Mike came back into the dining room. "Well, you have to give the Johnstons credit for their persistence, Chris," he said, sitting down beside her. "They made it impossible for us to say no. Your mother's finalizing the shipping arrangements."

Christina gave her father a hug. She could hardly believe it. She and Star were going to California!

5

"LADIES AND GENTLEMEN, IN PREPARATION FOR LANDING, please make sure that your seat belts are fastened. . . ."

Christina awoke to the flight attendant's announcement. Lifting her head from her tray table, she smiled when she noticed the blue pen marks on her fingers. She had spent most of the flight trying to write a note to Melanie. The words had sounded okay before she fell asleep, but now, as she reread the note, she wasn't so sure.

I know you love Image as much as I love Star, and you've probably been dreaming of the Triple Crown as long as I have. But over the past few days, I've decided that I can't let Derby fever take over my life. I'm not going to get so competitive that I can't be honest with you.

So here's the truth: I don't think that I interfered with

58

Raven during the Lafayette. I didn't use my crop during the early part of the race because I was supposed to be holding Callie back. However, I should have tried to talk with you about it after the race. I should have listened to your side of the story.

I know the next couple of months are going to be crazy for all of us. But I hope that no matter what happens to Star and Image, we'll always be friends.

With a sigh, Christina folded the note and stuffed it into her backpack. She would e-mail it to Melanie once she got to Dreamflight, the Johnstons' farm. She hoped Melanie would understand.

Looking out the window as the plane landed, Christina saw the southern California landscape below. Los Angeles spread out before her, a sprawling mass of buildings, houses, and freeways slightly obscured by smog. It was so different from the rolling green fields of Kentucky.

A wave of panic gripped Christina. Why had she insisted on bringing Star to this new place? Had she done the right thing? Suddenly she longed for the familiarity of Kentucky and the Keeneland track, despite the tension she had left behind.

"Are you continuing on to San Francisco with us, miss?" a flight attendant asked, snapping Christina out of her daze.

Embarrassed, Christina looked around and realized that everyone else was filing out of the plane. Grabbing her luggage from the overhead compartment, she hurried down the aisle.

There was a crush of people at the gate, and Christina pushed her way through the crowd. The Johnstons had told her that their assistant trainer would meet her at the gate, but how in the world would anyone find her in such chaos?

A petite woman with long brown hair approached her. "Are you Christina Reese?"

Christina nodded.

"I'm Deborah Easton, the assistant trainer at Dreamflight. Welcome to California."

Christina shook Deborah's hand, glad that the trainer had recognized her.

"Did you check any luggage?" Deborah asked.

"No, I managed to fit everything in these two bags," Christina replied. She shifted her duffel bag to a more comfortable position on her shoulder.

"Great. Baggage claim at LAX is a zoo. Besides, I'm double-parked," Deborah said, and winked at her.

Christina smiled shyly, thinking that she was going to like Deborah. She seemed more relaxed than Patrick and Amanda. "Is it always this crowded here?" she asked.

"Actually, it gets a lot worse. You're lucky that you didn't fly in during rush hour." Deborah pulled out her keys, which were attached to a tarnished snaffle bit keychain.

"Is Dreamflight far from the airport?" Christina said as they got into Deborah's dark green Jeep. She tossed her luggage into the backseat, on top of a bag of feed. "Sorry. My California geography isn't that great."

"Well, I probably couldn't tell you anything about Kentucky except where Churchill Downs is, so we're even," Deborah said. "We should be home in under an hour, assuming that we don't hit traffic."

During the drive, Deborah gave Christina a quick tour of the area, pointing out UCLA and the Getty Center, a museum specializing in classical art. "You'll have to go see the sights if you have time," Deborah told her.

"What about Santa Anita? Where's that?" Christina asked. The highway was so crowded with buildings, there couldn't possibly be a racetrack anywhere nearby.

"Oh, that's east of here. It's about an hour away from Dreamflight, which is in Old Agoura." Deborah laughed at the bewildered expression on Christina's face. "Don't worry about figuring out where everything is. We'll make sure you don't get lost. Besides, from what I've heard from Amanda and Patrick, it sounds like you'll be spending most of your time with your horse. He's a beautiful animal."

"How is he?" Christina wondered. She had been worried about Star ever since he flew to California on Monday. Star had never been on a plane before, and she didn't know how he'd react.

"I think he likes the farm. We gave him a roomy corner stall, and he sticks his head over the door whenever someone comes in."

Christina smiled. "And how's Callie?"

"He's being his usual skittish self," Deborah replied with a chuckle. "That colt frets away so much energy, I'm amazed he can still run. When we put him in a turnout, he runs up and down the fence, digging ruts in the dirt."

"Well, maybe his new training program will give him something else to think about," Christina said.

"I hope so," Deborah said, flicking on her turn signal. "This is our exit."

After getting off the freeway, Deborah drove down several smaller, winding streets. Christina watched as the rows of buildings gave way to houses and fields.

At last Deborah drove over a small bridge, and at the top of a hill they passed a stone sign with the words *Dreamflight Racing Farm*. Christina's eyes widened as she got a panoramic view of the facilities.

Of all the training complexes she'd ever seen, this was among the most beautiful. Red buildings with

Spanish-style roofs were scattered in the valley between two golden hills.

"So, what do you think?" Deborah asked.

"I can't wait to see everything up close," Christina replied, unable to stop staring. "How long have the Johnstons been here?"

"About four years. When they decided to start training on their own, Patrick and Amanda found this place. Supposedly some businessman paid to build it and then went bankrupt before it was completed." Deborah slowly steered down the dirt drive, passing several paddocks full of grazing horses. "So I assume you'll want to visit your horse before you unpack?"

"Definitely," Christina said. "If that's not too much trouble."

"Not at all. I have some horses I want to check on myself." Deborah parked her car by the largest barn. "This is our training barn. Normally all the stalls are full, but most of our horses are at Santa Anita right now. Your horse is in the last stall on the left."

Christina opened the car door and hurried down the aisle. She barely heard the stamps and nickers of the other horses as she walked past them.

Star whinnied excitedly when he heard Christina's footsteps. When Christina saw Star's head poking over the stall door, she sprinted to him and threw her arms around his neck. "Hey, boy! I've missed you so much." She buried her face in the horse's soft mane. Star breathed gentle hay-scented breaths onto her back.

After a moment Christina stepped back and looked at her horse carefully. His copper coat glistened in the light that filtered through the barn's windows. His eyes were clear and bright, and his ears were pricked happily. Christina breathed a sigh of relief. The trip hadn't affected him at all. And now that they were in California, she could devote all her energy to getting him ready for the Triple Crown. "I can't wait to ride you again," Christina said, giving Star another hug. The colt nudged her.

"Sorry, no treats," Christina apologized. When Star nudged her again, she laughed. "Did you really expect me to keep carrots in my pocket during such a long plane ride?"

Star bobbed his head.

"Oh, you're so spoiled," she said. "But I love you anyway, boy."

Christina heard another familiar nicker across the aisle. She turned to see Callie jerking his head up and down and kicking his stall door. After saying a quick good-bye to Star, Christina walked toward Callie.

"So now I see what Deborah means about you

going crazy in your stall," she commented, stroking Callie's forehead.

"Yeah, he's a nutcase," Deborah said, walking up. She checked the latch on his stall door. "But when he channels that nervous energy into running, he can be pretty amazing."

Christina nodded, remembering Callie's burst of speed in the Lafayette Stakes.

"I'm going down to the track so I can watch some of the afternoon workouts. Do you want me to take you up to your room first?" Deborah asked.

"No, that's all right. I want to see the track," Christina replied. She followed Deborah down an incline to the mile-long dirt oval. The track was similar to Whitebrook's except that the grass around it was golden rather than a lush green. However, someone had planted a row of trees around the oval, so a ribbon of dark green surrounded the track.

From a distance, Christina could see a boy riding a rambunctious gray colt. The horse bucked several times as he rounded the turn.

"That's Aaron Evans, one of our best exercise riders," Deborah said. "And the gray fireball he's riding is Blue Streak, one of our two-year-olds."

Christina watched the pair as they rode past on the rail. The intensity in the rider's brown eyes caught

Christina's attention. She had often been told that when she rode, she looked as if she was shutting out the rest of the world and its distractions. Aaron looked the same way.

Aaron smiled as he passed them. The smile softened all the features on his face, balancing his stubborn jawline.

Realizing that she was staring, Christina shook herself and looked away. But she couldn't help admitting that Aaron was cute.

Aaron guided Blue Streak around the track once more, trying to keep the Thoroughbred under control. They had just started down the homestretch when a gust of wind blew a clump of dirt and leaves against the colt's chest.

Blue Streak spun around, looking for the invisible assailant. Christina watched in alarm as the gray reared, sending Aaron sliding down his back. Aaron landed by the rail as Blue Streak galloped away.

Instantly Deborah was running toward the fallen rider. "Are you all right?" she called.

Aaron sat up slowly. The wind carried his answer Christina's way. "I'm fine," he replied with a weak chuckle.

Relieved that Aaron was okay, Christina hurried to catch Blue Streak. The colt was weaving up and down the rail at a gallop, still spooked. However, Christina could tell he was tiring. His swerves were becoming less frequent, and his strides were steadier.

Standing near the middle of the track, Christina positioned herself in the horse's path. Knowing that she was dealing with an unpredictable animal, she was prepared to dart to either side. But she hoped her presence would distract Blue Streak. It worked. Blue Streak came to a sliding halt several feet in front of her and eyed her warily, breathing hard.

"Hey, silly horse. I think you gave everyone a bit of a scare," Christina said gently as she reached out to take the horse's reins. The horse backed up several steps, but she held the reins firmly until he stopped fighting her grip. Christina led Blue Streak in several large circles before walking him back to Deborah and the fallen rider.

"Thanks for catching him, Christina," Deborah said, watching the horse's walk for any signs of injury. "Christina, this is Aaron."

"Nice to meet you." Christina reached down to shake Aaron's hand. The rider was still sitting on the track, catching his breath.

Aaron smiled up at her. There was dirt between his teeth. "Do I know how to make a first impression or what?" he joked. He ran a hand through his wind-tousled brown hair. "And I was planning to ask you if I could try out that colt of yours."

67

"You can ride Star anytime," Christina answered, wondering why his smile made her heart beat faster. "He's nowhere near as jumpy as this guy here."

"Well, Blue Streak and I are going to try this again," Aaron said. He used the railing to pull himself up. When he put weight on his left foot, though, the color drained from his face.

Deborah steadied him. "What's wrong?"

"I think I might have twisted my ankle." Pain softened Aaron's voice. "Give me a sec."

"I'll go get some ice," Deborah said. "Maybe we should take you to the hospital."

Aaron shook his head. "I'll be fine. Just let me get back on. We can't end things on that note." He put his left foot on the ground again and cursed under his breath as his leg buckled.

"You're in no shape to ride," Deborah insisted.

"I'll work him," Christina offered, even though she wasn't dressed for riding. She had worn a nice pair of jeans and her sneakers on the plane.

Deborah looked at her questioningly for a second. "Well, if you could manage Callie, you should be able to handle Blue Streak." She took the colt's reins. "Just take him around once at a canter and then we'll cool him out."

"No problem," Christina said. She adjusted the stirrups, then swung herself into the saddle. Blue

Streak immediately leaped sideways, but Christina managed to keep her balance. She cued the colt into a canter, trying to learn his rhythm. The young horse's strides were choppy as he moved down the track, and he took the turns wide, a sure sign that he was still green. However, he responded to Christina's commands, and she had no trouble holding him in check.

After Christina had circled the track, she trotted back to Deborah, who was standing beside a dark-haired young woman. Aaron was slowly limping up the hill.

"Great job, Christina. He looked nice out there," Deborah said. "Jessica, can you cool him out?"

The groom took Blue Streak's reins. "Welcome to Dreamflight," Jessica said.

"Thanks," Christina replied. She dismounted. "You're a good horse once you decide to run forward rather than sideways," she said, patting Blue Streak.

"You can say that again," Deborah agreed. "To be honest, I was a little doubtful when Patrick and Amanda told me you were riding Callie, because you're so young. But now I see that they made a great choice. You have a way with horses."

"It was nothing," Christina said modestly. "Aaron got all the bucks out of Blue Streak before I got on."

"Well, I know Aaron was glad you could step in," Deborah said. "Now, I'd better let you go change and unpack. You'll be staying in the guest room in my house. Patrick and Amanda left a list of instructions for Callie's training on your desk."

"I'll look at them right away," Christina said. "When are we taking Callie and Star to Santa Anita?"

"The Johnstons figured they should go up on Monday. The San Felipe Stakes will be run next Friday—that's Callie's race. And you're running Star in the Santa Anita Derby, which is the next day," Deborah answered. "Think you'll be ready?"

Christina nodded eagerly. A few days earlier, the prospect of preparing two horses for big stakes races in only one week would have been daunting. But now that she was in California, away from all her worries at home, she felt ready to face the challenge. "I can't wait," she said.

6

"CHRISTINA, COULD YOU WORK SOME EXTRA HORSES THIS morning?" Deborah asked the next morning. "I want Aaron to give his ankle a day off, and all of our other riders are at Santa Anita."

"Sure," Christina replied. She stood up in Star's stall and brushed the bedding from her breeches. Because of the three-hour time difference between Kentucky and California, she had woken up especially early. Unable to go back to sleep, she had gone out to the barn to sit in Star's stall and read. "Can I work Star first?"

"Sure. I'll have Jessica tack him up for you."

"That's okay. I can do it," Christina said. She enjoyed spending the extra time with her horse. "Which horse do you want me to ride after I finish with Star?"

"Probably Callie." The trainer glanced at her watch. "I'm going to go check in with Amanda and Patrick before they start their morning workouts. I'll see you at the track."

Star pranced eagerly in the crossties while Christina tacked him up. "Yeah, I bet you're eager to run, boy," Christina said as she bridled the horse. "It's been a few days, hasn't it? Maybe all that time off will help you run faster."

Star snorted and continued to dance in place as Christina fastened his noseband and put on her helmet and a pair of gloves.

"Stop being so impatient, silly. We're going, okay?" Christina began leading Star toward the training track. As she walked, Christina couldn't help comparing the quiet of Dreamflight with the tense atmosphere at Keeneland.

Aaron was standing on the rail when they reached the track. Christina waved. "Hey, Aaron. How's your ankle?"

"It's fine," Aaron said quickly. "I wanted to ride today, but Deborah wouldn't let me. Are the trainers you work for so overprotective?"

"Given that my parents are training Star, yes," Christina replied with a smile.

"Oh, yeah, I forgot. You're Ashleigh Griffen's daughter, right?" he asked.

Christina nodded. Not a week went by when someone didn't ask her that question. When she had first gotten her license, Christina found it hard to follow in her mother's footsteps. Although she was proud of her mother, Christina had wanted to prove herself on her own terms. Now that she and Star had made a name for themselves, Christina no longer worried about living in her mother's shadow.

"I bet the media loves the fact that you're riding the son of your mother's prized racehorse," Aaron said.

Christina rolled her eyes. "Don't get me started," she mumbled. "Could you hold Star for me while I get on?"

Aaron nodded and took the reins. "Mind if I stay and watch you work him?"

"Go for it." Christina vaulted into Star's saddle. "We're not doing anything too interesting, though. Just a jog and a slow gallop."

"Don't worry. I'm sure it will be more exciting than studying for my calculus test," Aaron joked.

Christina laughed as she eased Star onto the track. She cued the horse into an extended trot and then a canter, checking to make sure he was still sound after the long trip. To her relief, the colt's strides were smooth and sure.

"I missed riding you, boy," Christina told her horse as they circled the track. "You know you're my favorite horse in the world, don't you?"

After a few laps at a canter, Christina cued Star into a steady, ground-eating gallop. The colt fought against her hold, wanting to move faster. Christina smiled, hoping that this meant Star was ready to show his true speed again. "I'll let you go as fast as you want tomorrow, all right?"

Star's ears flicked back at the sound of her voice. "That's right, we'll show California what Whitebrook horses can do."

By the time Christina finished working Star, Deborah was standing at the rail. Beside her a blond-haired groom was holding Callie's reins.

"Your horse looks good," Deborah commented when Christina rode up to her.

"I think he likes it here," Christina said. She leaned down to pat her colt before dismounting. "Thanks for getting Callie out for me."

The groom handed her Callie's reins. "You're welcome. I'm Anisa, by the way."

Christina tried to shake Anisa's hand, but Callie thrust his nose in the way.

Both she and Anisa laughed. "He's full of himself this morning," Anisa warned.

"Then I guess I'll have to work him extra hard," Christina said. She turned to look at the horse. "You're going to be good for me, aren't you?"

"Callie doesn't know the meaning of that word,"

Deborah joked. "I'm sure he'll try to pull your arms out during your work."

Christina nodded, remembering how hard it had been to restrain Callie as the colt leaned into the bit during the Lafayette. "What do you want me to do?"

"Not too much. The Johnstons want you to take him out for a long canter on the trails this afternoon to build up his stamina," Deborah replied. "For now, let's just warm him up at a jog, then do a two-furlong breeze."

When Christina had read the Johnstons' training schedule the previous night, she had been surprised that the trainers wanted to breeze Callie so soon. But she knew better than to question them.

Despite Anisa's and Deborah's warnings, Callie behaved himself during the warm-ups. He threw a couple of bucks at the beginning, testing Christina's ability to keep him in check, but when Christina kept her hold, he settled down.

At Deborah's signal, Christina slid her hands up Callie's neck and cried, "Go!" The horse needed no more encouragement. He sprang forward.

Christina felt the power in each of Callie's bounding strides as they quickly worked the quarter mile. She wished she could combine Callie's amazing early speed with Star's incredible endurance and closing kick.

Deborah looked pleased when Christina rode back to her. "I've never seen him so well behaved." She showed Christina the colt's time. "He's such a great sprinter that I almost wish Amanda wasn't making him try longer distances," she said. "Do you think he'll be able to make the transition?"

"As long as he doesn't burn himself out early in the race," Christina answered. "He hates being restrained. But we might be able to change that."

"I hope so." Deborah patted the colt, then said, "I want to work six others this morning. Think you can handle that?"

"Definitely," Christina said. "Let's go."

The combined effects of waking up so early and exercising so many of Dreamflight's horses finally caught up with Christina as she rode Callie back from the trails that afternoon. Her shoulders ached from keeping tight holds on all the overeager two-year-olds, and her leg muscles were cramping. She couldn't wait to go back to Deborah's house and take a nap.

"So, did Callie behave himself on the trails?"

Aaron's voice startled both Christina and Callie. She had to react quickly as the colt pulled on the reins, half dragging her.

"Sorry about that," Aaron apologized.

76

Christina murmured soothingly to Callie. "Any idea why he's so high-strung?" she asked.

Aaron shrugged. "He's always been like that. The Johnstons tend to like spirited horses. Matter of Time is a monster at the gate. It usually takes three attendants to drag him in." He smiled. "But I guess I don't need to tell you that after you exercised all the young ones this morning."

"They're lots of fun, though," Christina said. "Hey, how did your calculus test go?"

"Well, it's over." Aaron leaned against the paddock railing. "I can't wait until my spring break starts next week."

"Where do you go to school?" Christina guessed that Aaron was a couple of years older than she was, but she wasn't sure.

"The local junior college for now. I'm taking some classes there and trying to get my jockey's license," Aaron replied. "You're lucky that you already have yours. The Johnstons have too many good jockeys clamoring to ride for them as it is."

"So why don't you go down to Santa Anita and try to get rides with other trainers?" Christina asked.

"You know what it's like at the track. Unless you have the right connections, it's impossible to get mounts. The Johnstons offered me a steady job at Dreamflight, so I figure I'll work here and get some experience first." Aaron pulled a carrot out of his pocket, bit off a piece, then fed the rest to Callie.

Christina didn't know what to say. She knew she was lucky that her parents were so well known in the industry. She had gotten the chance to ride incredible horses from the beginning, so it had been easier for her to show other trainers what she could do.

As Aaron continued talking about his riding career, Christina was surprised that he didn't seem upset about not having his license or getting top mounts. He didn't have the usual cutthroat competitiveness that most other riders had. After her recent experience with Melanie at Keeneland, Christina wasn't sure that was a bad thing.

"What about you? Any plans for college?" Aaron asked.

"I'm taking a year off so that I can focus on Star. Then I'll go to the University of Kentucky at Lexington." It had been hard for Christina to convince her parents to let her take some time off. She had won the argument only by promising she would go back to school after one year. Christina started to say more, but Callie tossed his head again. "I'd better get him back to his stall before he goes crazy," she said. "I guess I'll see you at the track tomorrow morning."

"Definitely. One day off from riding is more than enough," Aaron said.

Christina turned Callie toward the barn, but when she heard Aaron's footsteps behind her, she paused and turned around.

"I was wondering if I could take you around L.A. sometime," Aaron said hesitantly. "It's your spring break—you should see some of the tourist stuff."

Christina watched Aaron uncertainly. Was he just being friendly, or was he asking her on a date? She had a feeling that she would enjoy spending time with Aaron, but it was too soon after her breakup with Parker for her to date anyone. "Um, I'll probably have to take Star on a trail ride for most of the afternoons," she began. Aaron's face fell. "But maybe we could try going somewhere this weekend," she added.

Aaron grinned. "That would be great. I'll start figuring out some fun things to do."

Aaron's words still lingered in Christina's mind when she got back to Deborah's house. She sank into the bed, folding her arms behind her head and staring at the ceiling. To distract herself, she considered Star's training. She hoped that coming to California had broken Star's habit of slacking off during the earlier parts of his breeze. If not, though, she would have to do something to change his running style.

Thinking about Star reminded Christina of her

promise to call home every day. She picked up the phone, hoping her parents would be there.

"Hello?" Christina recognized Melanie's voice.

Christina decided to play it cool, hoping that her cousin would be ready to talk. "Hey, Mel. It's Christina. How are things at Whitebrook?"

"Hi, Chris." Melanie's voice was softer than usual. "I got your e-mail."

Christina twisted the phone cord in her hand, leaving imprints in her palm, as she waited for her cousin to continue.

"You're right. We can't let all the competition in the air come between us," Melanie said. "Maybe it would be best if we didn't talk about racing at all."

Christina leaned her head against the wall, considering the idea. It wasn't the reconciliation she wanted, but it was better than nothing. "What else can we talk about?" she asked. "I don't think we've had a conversation not related to horses in years."

"Well, we could talk about boys," Melanie replied with her old playfulness.

"Like Jazz Taylor?" Christina teased. The handsome lead singer of the band Pegasus owned half of Image, and it was easy to see that Melanie was interested in him.

"I was thinking more along the lines of Parker

Townsend. I never heard what he said to you after Katie's party," Melanie said.

Christina inhaled sharply. "Mel, Parker and I decided to break up for real." It hurt to say the words.

Melanie was silent for a moment. Then she said, "I'm so sorry, Chris."

"It's okay. We both agreed that with the way things were going lately, we would have ended up hurting each other," Christina replied.

"Are you sure you're all right?" Melanie asked.

"Well, I try not to think about it," Christina admitted with a sigh. "I know we did the right thing, but I can't help wondering if things could have worked out differently."

"You're going to be okay," Melanie assured her. "You remember how upset I was when Kevin broke up with me? I threw myself into riding so I wouldn't have to think about it. And eventually I realized it was for the best." Melanie paused. "So I guess now wouldn't be a good time for me to ask if there are any cute guys in California."

Aaron came to Christina's mind, but she didn't say anything at first.

"Okay, Chris. I know that silence means there *is* someone. Hey, come on, spill," Melanie urged.

Christina laughed at her cousin's directness. "Well,

there's this exercise rider named Aaron," she said. "He offered to show me around the city."

"You should take him up on it. There's tons of stuff to do in L.A. I went there with Dad a couple of years ago." Melanie's father was a record producer who spent most of his time traveling.

"I don't know," Christina said. She picked up a pen and started doodling on the pad by the phone. "It almost sounded like he was asking me out on a date. And I'm not ready for that." After drawing a few more circles and stars, Christina deliberately changed the subject. "Have you heard from Katie and the others?"

"Yeah. Barbara called from Hawaii yesterday," Melanie said. "They're having a blast. They can see whales breaching from the window of the condo."

For a moment Christina almost wished she were with her friends in Hawaii. But as soon as she thought about why she wasn't there—because she was getting Star ready to race in the Kentucky Derby—she knew she wouldn't change a thing.

"Okay, I think your mom wants to talk to you," Melanie said. "But before you go, Chris, I want to say one race-related thing to you."

"What is it?"

Melanie took a deep breath. "I watched a replay of the Lafayette. You were right. You weren't using your crop when you passed us. I guess Raven just flinched because she hates it when horses kick dirt at her. I'm sorry. I never should have accused you of deliberately interfering with me. I know you would never do that."

"Don't worry about it," Christina said, surprised to realize she no longer cared about the incident.

"But I think I might have made it up to you with what I said to Brad today," Melanie said, her voice mischievous. "He was giving me a hard time about Image, so I pointed out to him that Celtic Mist doesn't have a very good track record against Whitebrook horses."

"You didn't!" Christina laughed at her cousin's boldness.

"Of course I did. Anyway, I hope that Star kicks Pocket Money's butt in the Santa Anita Derby, Chris."

"And I hope Image makes Celtic Mist eat her dust." Christina knew she would have to choose her words carefully whenever she talked with Melanie about Image now, but she was glad they were friends again.

After saying good-bye to Melanie, Christina gave her mother an update on how Star was doing. Knowing that Ashleigh was still concerned that going to California had been a mistake, Christina focused on how happy Star was in his new surroundings.

"Well, you've always known what's best for Star," Ashleigh said after Christina told her about the morning work. "It looks like we're going to be pretty busy here at Keeneland. I don't think I'll be able to fly out until the morning of the Santa Anita Derby. So I'm relying on you to keep Star on target for his race."

"Don't worry, Mom. I'm going to spend almost every second from now until next Saturday getting Star ready," Christina promised.

By the time she said good-bye to her mother, Christina could hardly keep her eyes open. She lay down to take a nap, but she couldn't stop herself from speculating about what was going on at Keeneland. Melanie's mention of Brad made her wonder what he was saying about her. He was probably telling everyone at Keeneland that she had brought Star to California because she was afraid of the competition in the Bluegrass. And the way gossip spread at the track, some people would believe him.

These thoughts strengthened Christina's resolve. *If Star wins the Santa Anita Derby, then no one can criticize us for coming to California*, she thought. Knowing this, Christina began thinking about Star's training schedule again. She went over breezes, workout times, and plans for afternoon trail rides until she finally fell asleep.

7

"EVERYTHING OKAY?" CHRISTINA ASKED AARON, KEEPING her eyes on the track. She was crouched over Star's withers as they waited to break from the training gate. In the next slot, Aaron was trying to keep Blue Streak from tearing down the door.

"Yeah. But Deborah had better let him run soon," Aaron replied.

Since Blue Streak had trouble settling in the gate without company, Christina had volunteered to breeze Star against the two-year-old. She hoped the racelike setting would prompt Star to a sharper start. So far it seemed to be working. Star's muscles tensed beneath her.

The bell rang, and the training gates slammed open. Blue Streak flinched, but Star surged ahead.

"Good boy!" Christina encouraged, feeling the power in each of the colt's strides. He was leaning into the bit, pushing forward on his own. She gave him a little more rein, rewarding him.

Star snatched up the excess rein, running gamely. Then, almost in midstride, he dropped the pace. Although he continued to move forward, his spectacular impulsion was gone.

Christina bit her lip to keep from screaming in frustration. She glanced over her shoulder. Blue Streak had recovered from his initial gate problems and was gaining on Star. "Come on, Star. We can't let him catch us," Christina urged.

But Star once again responded only halfheartedly. Blue Streak drew even with Star, and Christina still couldn't get her horse to move faster. It wasn't until Blue Streak got a half length ahead that Star finally decided to start moving again.

Christina looked to her right. Now that Star was running at his full potential, Blue Streak didn't stand a chance. By the quarter pole, Star had managed to pull ahead by a neck. Still, the finish didn't make Christina feel any better. If Star had kept his mind on the breeze, he would have won by several lengths.

"I wish you could tell me why you're running like this," Christina murmured as she slowed Star down. She had been hoping that Star's slow breezes were mostly her fault—that he had been sensing her distress over the tension at Keeneland and it was affecting his running style. But they were away from all that now, and Star was still having difficulties. "What's the problem, boy?" Christina asked.

Aaron trotted alongside her. "Does Star always wait for other horses to catch him before he decides to run?"

Christina shook his head. "I don't know what's gotten into him lately. In his last race he stayed in front almost the whole time."

"Yeah. I saw the Louisiana Derby on TV. He ran such an amazing race. Still, you can't forget that he made up a length in a hundred yards. And Blue Streak was trying his hardest."

"But the competition will be tougher in the Santa Anita Derby. Star can't slack off early on if he wants to win," Christina said. She pulled her horse down to a walk and leaned on his neck, not minding the way his copper mane got tangled in her own hair. She sighed, hoping she could change Star's running style before it was too late.

Christina smiled contentedly as she walked Star through a small grove of trees later that afternoon. The maze of trails at Dreamflight spread out over the golden rolling hills, and the paths stretched on for miles. Star seemed to be enjoying himself. He lifted his legs higher, trotting eagerly between the trees. Christina had to dodge several lower branches as Star jogged toward the small creek at the edge of the Dreamflight property.

Christina stopped Star on the bank of the creek, letting the colt drink. Although she was having fun, she knew that she had to get down to business. She had to find a way to make Star focus from the beginning to the end of his breezes.

After Star's workout, Christina had paged her parents at Keeneland to ask for their advice. Ashleigh had been only slightly concerned by Christina's description of how Star had waited for Blue Streak to catch up. To make Christina feel better, she had told a story about how Fleet Goddess, one of the mares at Whitebrook, had done the same thing during her racing days.

"If you're really concerned about it, you could always carry a crop when you ride," Ashleigh had suggested, echoing Mike's earlier advice.

"But you know how Star hates being treated roughly," Christina pointed out.

"It isn't rough treatment if you don't use the whip in anger," Ashleigh replied. "You carry a crop with most of your other horses."

"Star's different," Christina insisted. She just couldn't risk losing the bond she had with her beloved horse.

"To be honest, I'm really not worried about Star's times," Ashleigh said. "But I can tell that it's worrying you. All I can say is that carrying a crop might help. It worked with Goddess."

Christina knew that the crop hadn't hurt her mother's relationship with Fleet Goddess. The beautiful dark bay mare always came to the front of her stall whenever she heard Ashleigh's voice. Still, as she was saddling Star for their trail ride, Christina had been reluctant to take a stick. Then she thought about her old eventing days. She had been hesitant to use a crop on Sterling Dream at first, but when she had finally done it, the mare had carried her to victory in their first event.

After they passed another stand of trees, Christina steered Star to the left. There was a level field beside the path, the perfect place for short gallops. Christina cantered Star in a big circle around the field, almost laughing in delight as the wind whipped through her hair. "Let's run!" she cried after settling into her jockey's crouch.

Star obeyed, and the trees became an indistinguishable blur of earth tones and shades of green. Christina stayed motionless over his neck, trying not to worry that Star would drop the pace.

Star slowed after the first furlong. Reluctantly Christina reached around to tap his flank with the crop.

Star leaped forward at the touch of the whip but kept his impulsion for only a few strides before slowing again. Christina flicked the crop in front of his eyes, the way she had done with Callie in the Lafayette. The colt accelerated, but his strides were uneven and jarring.

"Don't do this now, Star," Christina begged her horse. "Please, just run for me like you did in Louisiana."

Star swished his tail in response.

Unwilling to let Star drop the pace, Christina used her whip several more times during the gallop. Each time the colt responded abruptly to her signals. But he made no effort to smooth out his strides, and his ears flicked distractedly. When Christina eased him down to a trot at the end of the field, she wondered if she had truly accomplished anything. She didn't want to spend the rest of Star's career whipping him every few furlongs to keep him going.

After Star had cooled down, Christina dismounted. She fed him an apple slice, then led him back to the creek.

"Remember Montana, boy?" she asked. "Everything was going wrong. You and I were having trouble communicating with each other. Then we got lost, and I had no idea how to get back to Lyssa's ranch. Something happened that night that brought you back to me. Maybe we need a little of that now," she mused, and leaned against the horse's shoulder.

"Since the moment you got better, I've dreamed of riding you in the Kentucky Derby. I want us to win the Triple Crown together, just like your half brother Wonder's Champion did. But if we're going to do that, you have to help me." Star lowered his head to munch on the grass, and Christina stroked his ears.

"You've never needed me to ask you to run before. What changed? I know you can win the Derby. You just need to concentrate." Christina took a step back and looked at Star, admiring his majestic frame. From his elegantly shaped head to his well-proportioned body and his long, straight legs, Star was a perfectly built Thoroughbred.

"You know how much I love you, right?" Christina fed Star another apple slice before preparing to mount again.

Star sidestepped as she tried to put her foot in the stirrup. Christina noticed him eyeing the crop she had stuck in her back pocket. "Easy, sweetie. I'm not using that anymore," she soothed, stroking Star's coat gently.

Christina tried mounting again, but Star kept moving away. Finally she balanced the crop on her saddle, where Star couldn't see it, and the colt allowed her to get on.

"What's wrong, Star? You haven't done that to me since we were in Montana," Christina said. She wondered whether it had been a good idea for her to bring the crop on the trails. On one hand, she wanted Star to think of these rides as fun rather than stressful. On the other, though, she had needed the crop to keep Star going.

As Christina made her way back to the barn, she let her mind wander. She couldn't help but imagine a nightmarish Derby scenario in which Star fell too far behind in the first half mile and couldn't make up the distance. She reached forward and rubbed Star's neck. "I'm not going to let that happen to us, Star," she insisted. "We've come too far to give up now."

"I talked with Aaron, and he's going to ride Dream-flight Duke, one of our five-year-olds, with you and Callie today," Deborah said when Christina stopped by her office on Saturday morning. "Do you want to work with Star first?"

"No, I'll get on Callie," Christina decided. "I could use a change of routine." She thought back to Callie's work the previous day. She had galloped the horse slowly over half a mile, ignoring the pain in her arms as he yanked at the reins. Riding Callie always felt so strange after pushing Star forward.

"Great. Just let Aaron know. I think he's helping Jessica with the morning chores." Deborah looked back down at the paperwork on her desk. "I'll be down there in ten minutes, assuming this mess doesn't eat me first."

Christina laughed. "Good luck with that," she said. She turned and saw Aaron and Jessica at the far end of the barn. They were pretending to fence with wooden rakes.

"So who's winning?" Christina asked as she walked up to them.

"Definitely me," Jessica replied. "Aaron's been disqualified because he's such a cheater!" She raised her rake to hit Aaron's again.

"Hey, it's not my fault I'm taller and stronger," Aaron retorted. "Grab something and join in." He gestured to the extra tools propped up in the aisle.

Unable to resist, Christina picked up a broom. "Girls against boys, right?"

"Of course," Jessica said.

Christina and Jessica easily overpowered Aaron, driving him backward down the aisle and startling several horses with their laughter. After they cornered him by the door, Aaron dropped his rake. He raised his arms in the air and made a scene out of calling, "I surrender!"

"Well, now that that's settled, I'm supposed to tell you that we're going to work Callie and Dreamflight Duke first this morning," Christina said.

"Cool. I think Anisa already has them groomed and saddled," Aaron replied. He leaned his rake against the barn door. "Do you need help with Star?"

"It's all right. I can take care of him."

"Oh, let Aaron help, Christina," Jessica said. Her light brown eyes twinkled with amusement. "He's just waiting for the perfect moment to ask if you want to go to Universal Studios this afternoon."

Aaron glared at Jessica and then hurried down the aisle toward Callie's stall, obviously embarrassed.

"Sorry, but I have to tease Aaron. We spend so much time together that he's practically like my brother," Jessica explained with a smile. "Since he always gives me a hard time when he sees me with a new guy, I figure he needs a taste of his own medicine. Seriously, though, he's great."

"Yeah, he seems nice," Christina said. Jessica reminded her of Melanie. Both the groom and her cousin were unafraid of speaking their minds. "Anyway, I'd better go get Star groomed so we don't keep Deborah waiting."

As Christina walked to Star's stall, she wondered what she should say to Aaron. She had to admit that she wanted to get to know him better. At home, Christina had formed few friendships with other jockeys at the tracks. Most of them were a lot older than she was, and having to compete against them made things even more complicated. But Aaron didn't have that same hard, competitive edge. It was difficult not to like him.

Still, it was too soon after her breakup with Parker to consider another relationship. Even though she and Parker had been drifting apart for so long that it was hard for her to remember their last happy moment together, Christina still wasn't over him. Besides, she didn't have time for a relationship at the moment. She had to focus on Star.

When Christina reached Star's stall, she was surprised to find Aaron saddling her horse. "He'll be ready in a minute," he said, not looking at her.

Christina let herself into the stall. "I'm surprised you managed to saddle him without crossties. How did you keep him still?"

"We have an arrangement. He can move all he wants as long as he lets me put his tack on." Aaron checked the girth. "Sorry about Jessica back there."

"Don't worry about it," Christina replied. "We all have friends like that."

Aaron grinned wryly. "She sure does know how to make a mess out of my timing. So, would you say yes if I invited you to Universal Studios?"

Christina knew she should tell Aaron the truth about Parker, but she had only known him for a few days. She opened her mouth to cite Star as an excuse to decline but wound up saying something else entirely. "I might be convinced," she said, smiling shyly.

Aaron's grin broadened. "What if I tell you about the really cool Jurassic Park ride? There's a drop that's over ten stories."

"Sounds like fun," Christina said, playing along even though she still wasn't sure it was a good idea.

"Okay, it's settled, then. We'll leave after the morning workouts. Now, let's get down to the track."

Deborah was standing at the track when they got there, holding a light chestnut horse. "This is Duke, one of the most solid horses on the farm," she told Christina. "I'm going to have Aaron keep him at a moderate pace. Your job is to make Callie go even slower."

"I'll try," Christina said. She let Aaron give her a leg up into the saddle. He boosted her up so high that she almost flew over the horse's side.

The exercise was easier said than done. Callie couldn't stand having another horse ahead of him. He tossed his head and leaned against the bit, fighting

Christina for every millimeter of rein. One of Christina's riding gloves tore during the struggle, yet she kept holding on, refusing to let the horse win the battle.

After six furlongs at a gallop, Christina's arms were aching so badly, she was about to fall forward onto Callie's neck. She sighed with relief when Deborah gave her the signal to pass Aaron and breeze the remaining quarter mile. To her surprise, Callie didn't respond with his usual surge. He increased his pace, but the typical burst of speed wasn't there. Fighting Christina had used up most of his energy.

"Not bad," Deborah said when Christina finished the gallop. "I could tell he was pulling your arms out, but he did manage some nice times toward the end."

Christina was glad that Deborah didn't seem discouraged by how hard Callie had been fighting her. Privately she wondered if Callie would have enough energy to run a whole race after struggling with her at the beginning. However, she reasoned that the Johnstons knew Callie better than she did, so she probably didn't have anything to worry about.

After she dismounted, Christina stretched the muscles in her arms and shoulders.

"It looked like he was giving you a hard time," Aaron observed. He was still walking Duke in small circles. In contrast to Callie, Duke was completely calm.

"Yeah. But he's always like that," Christina answered. "Getting on Star will be a nice change." She looked over at Aaron and Duke again and suddenly had an idea for Star's workout. "Aaron, could you do me a favor and ride Duke next to me when I work Star?"

Aaron nodded. "As long as it's okay with Deborah."

The trainer gave her permission. As she warmed Star up, Christina considered her strategy for the colt's half-mile breeze. Not wanting to discuss the disastrous trail ride, she hadn't called her parents the previous evening for more advice. She was on her own for this workout.

At the half-mile marker, Christina stopped Star and motioned for Aaron to join her. "Let Duke run as fast as he can," she instructed. "I'm going to try keeping Star ahead of you."

"After seeing Star run yesterday, I don't think he'll have any trouble kicking dirt in our faces," Aaron observed confidently.

"I hope so." Christina noticed the whip Aaron was carrying. After debating with herself for a moment, she asked, "Can I borrow your crop?"

"Uh, sure." Aaron handed it over to her. Star saw it out of the corner of his eye and pranced to the left, almost hitting the rail before Christina got him under control. "Why do you want to use it? He looked like he was running pretty well on his own."

"I don't plan to show it to Star unless he starts slacking off," Christina said defensively. "I just need to keep his attention." Without waiting for Aaron's response, Christina positioned herself in Star's saddle. She waved across the field to let Deborah know they were ready, then waited for Deborah's hand to drop before letting Star accelerate.

Within the first five strides, Star distanced himself from Duke. Remembering Lyssa's visualization strategy, Christina tried her hardest to picture Star having the perfect breeze, instead of thinking about all that had gone wrong lately. The strategy seemed to be working. Star easily opened up a strong lead over Duke.

Soon Star lost his focus again. He took the far turn wide and began to slow his gallop. Before he could slow too much, Christina flicked the whip in front of his eyes and then hit his shoulder with it. "Please, Star, don't do this," she pleaded.

But once again Star reacted badly to the crop. He tried to swing even farther to the outside, even ignoring Christina's leg signals. Seeing an opening, Aaron moved Duke between Star and the rail. Christina could hear the pounding of the other horse's hooves coming closer and closer. "Okay, Star. You really need to kick in now." She reluctantly used the whip again, not knowing what else to do.

Star drifted even farther to the outside. His sideways gallop was ragged. Desperately Christina glanced up the track. There was only one furlong left. She couldn't let Star lose! Pulling hard on her inside rein to get the colt's attention, Christina used her whip several more times down the stretch. Star accelerated, though his stride became more uneven with each tap of the whip. In the end, Star managed to pass Deborah with his head just in front of Duke's. But it was hardly the breeze of a champion. His gallop lacked any sort of rhythm, and the half-mile work had left him sweating and blowing hard.

Frustrated, Christina could feel the sting of tears as Star broke to a canter without fighting her. Things had gotten worse instead of better.

"What happened out there?" Aaron asked as he drew even with her.

Christina shook her head. "I don't want to talk about it," she mumbled, hoping Aaron would take the hint.

"Maybe you shouldn't worry about his tendency to play around so much," Aaron suggested hesitantly. "He seemed a lot happier on the track yesterday than he did today."

Christina glared at Aaron. She knew how to train Star without his help!

Seeing Christina's expression, Aaron quickly apologized. "I didn't mean to tell you what to do," he said. "I just wish you wouldn't worry so much."

"Well, I have to worry!" Christina snapped, unable to hold her temper in check any longer. "The Santa Anita Derby is a week from today, and we're leaving for Santa Anita on Monday. I have to make things work and show everyone that I made the right choice in bringing Star to California!"

Aaron didn't reply.

"I want to spend the afternoon on the trails with Star now," Christina told him. "I guess I'll have to see Universal Studios some other time." Then she turned Star around so she wouldn't have to keep talking to Aaron.

But as she took Star back to the barn, Christina wondered how on earth she was going to make things better. She had tried almost every technique she knew. What else could she do?

8

ON MONDAY MORNING CHRISTINA WOKE BEFORE SUNRISE. She wandered around Dreamflight listlessly, dreading the upcoming day. The scene on Sunday morning had been a repeat of what had happened on Saturday— only this time Star had behaved even worse, finishing his breeze with such slow fractions that she had lied to her parents when they asked about his time.

Desperate for advice, Christina had asked Deborah for her opinion. However, all Deborah had said was that Star was having an off week and would be fine once they got to the track. Like her parents, the trainer had advised her to relax and stop worrying.

Christina had thought about calling Ian or Cindy to discuss Star's problems, but she was afraid they would relay her concerns to her parents. Her parents had been so reluctant to let her come to California in the first place that she didn't want them to suspect anything was wrong. If she told them how she had messed things up, it would be like admitting that she couldn't train Star without them watching her every move.

Christina leaned against the barn door and closed her eyes. She let herself remember Star's Louisiana Derby run, smiling as she thought about how in tune with her horse she had been then. What had happened?

"Good morning, Christina." Aaron's voice jerked Christina back to the present.

Christina's opened her eyes. "Good morning," she replied coolly. Since their conversation on the track Saturday, she and Aaron had been avoiding each other.

"Deborah was wondering if you could jog Callie before we get him ready for the van ride," Aaron said.

"That's fine. I wasn't planning to work Star today anyway," Christina said. She didn't want him to stress his legs before the two-hour trip to the track at Santa Anita. "How many horses are going?"

"Pretty much everyone who's sound. There are some good maiden races toward the end of the Santa Anita meet that Patrick and Amanda wanted to try," Aaron answered.

"So are you, Jessica, and Anisa going to Santa Anita, too?"

"I am, but the grooms are staying here to look after things."

Christina tried not to look disappointed. Without Jessica and Anisa there, whom was she going to talk to when she wasn't working with the horses? "When are we leaving?"

"After lunch. Do you need any help with Star?" Aaron offered.

Christina shook her head. "I'll be fine." Since Saturday, she had started doing everything for Star, spending extra time with her horse in hopes that the answer to all his problems would suddenly pop into her head. So far, inspiration hadn't hit.

By noon Christina was regretting her decision not to ask for help. Jogging Callie had taken more time than she had expected. The Dreamflight colt wasn't going well for her, either. He fought Christina's restraint more and more with each passing breeze, and his sweating and pawing started the moment he laid eyes on the track.

Deborah was concerned about Callie's new attitude. However, the trainer told Christina that the Johnstons had made it clear that she needed to follow their training schedule. Personally, Christina had a feeling that the schedule was hurting Callie's chances of becoming a distance horse, but she wasn't in a position to question the Johnstons' decisions. The only decisions she could second-guess were the ones she made involving Star.

After she finished hosing Callie down and rubbing his legs with liniment, Christina ran to Star's stall and dug around in his tack trunk for the shipping wraps.

Star stamped impatiently as she wrapped his legs. "Yeah, I know you're excited about going to the track, boy. But you have to stand still or else we're going to keep everyone waiting." She could hear Deborah's voice as she directed the other Dreamflight horses into the van. The flighty two-year-olds were giving her trouble.

Anisa stopped by Star's stall door on her way to the van. "Everything okay in there?" the blond-haired groom wondered.

"Yeah, I'm just having one of those bad wrapping days," Christina said, straightening a fold in one of the blue wraps.

Anisa laughed, grabbed a set of wraps, and started the last leg. "So should I put some money on Star this coming weekend?" she asked.

Christina had seen the early odds for the race. The West Coast champion Pocket Money was the three-to-two favorite, and Star was a distant four-to-one second choice. Normally she would have had complete confidence in her horse, but after what had happened over the past couple of days, she wasn't so sure. "Well, I'm not exactly the most unbiased person to ask, you know," she said, avoiding the question.

"Maybe not, but Aaron keeps telling me that you're the best rider he's ever seen. And he's seen lots of riders come through Dreamflight."

Christina blushed. She couldn't believe that Aaron still admired her riding after he'd seen her recent workouts.

"But then again, I don't think Aaron's unbiased, either," Anisa added. "I hope you've realized that he likes you."

Christina could feel herself turning redder by the moment. She gave her leg wrap far more attention than it deserved. "He's a sweet guy," she said at last.

"Well, if I were you, I'd go for it," Anisa advised. "He was pretty hurt when you changed your mind about Universal Studios."

"I had to work with Star," Christina said. There was a defensive edge to her voice.

"I know, but you won't be able to do trail work at Santa Anita. So you should sneak away from the track and have some fun," Anisa insisted, finishing her wrap. "Just consider it, okay?" With that, Anisa hurried out to the van, not giving Christina a chance to argue.

Not wanting to think about Aaron, Christina quickly led Star to the van. The colt pranced at the end of his lead line, his ears pricked.

For a moment Christina smiled. At least Star still seemed excited about going to the track. But her smile faded as she continued to worry about his track performance.

"We're ready for Star," Christina heard Deborah call from inside the van.

Star loaded without too much fuss, only hesitating once on the ramp, while Callie needed a whole bag of carrots to coax him in.

After making sure her horse was comfortable, Christina climbed into the cab of the luxury horse van, sitting on the passenger seat beside Deborah. Aaron was driving his own car. He had offered Christina a ride, but she had declined, unable to forget what Anisa had just told her and not wanting to feel pressured into making promises that she couldn't keep.

The journey to Santa Anita was a slow one. There was an accident on one of the freeways, and the stop-and-go traffic made Christina dizzy.

At last Santa Anita Park came into view. Christina had never been to this track, and she marveled at its majesty. From a distance, the green grass and white fences provided a startling contrast to the silhouette of mountains in the background. The grandstands weren't quite as large as those of Churchill Downs, but the track was more modern than Keeneland.

Patrick and Amanda Johnston met them in the

parking lot. As usual, Amanda looked perfectly put together, this time wearing a pastel blouse and a flower-print skirt. Christina remembered a lecture her mother had given her a few weeks earlier about dressing nicely at the track. She knew Ashleigh would love it if she dressed like Amanda.

"Hi, Christina," Patrick said after he had spoken with Deborah. "How's Callie been doing?"

"Well, we've been following your schedule," Christina replied. She had done everything that the Johnstons wanted, but she couldn't see them liking the results.

"I guess we'll see the results tomorrow morning, then," Amanda said. "I figure we'll work Callie first thing. That way he'll be done before most of the reporters and spectators arrive."

"Sounds good. Now I'd better get Star unloaded." Christina forced herself to smile so that she wouldn't betray her nervousness about the next day's breeze.

However, as Christina got Star settled into the roomy stall the Johnstons had reserved for him, all she could think about was how the trainers would react the next morning when they saw Callie run. And the only thought that worried her more than Callie having a disastrous breeze was the prospect of working Star.

● ● ●

"Okay, Callie. I know things haven't been going well lately, but I really need your help today," Christina said as she completed a lap around the track at a canter.

She blinked several times, trying to clear her mind. She had tossed and turned in her motel room all night, worrying about both Callie and Star. Callie was the whole reason the Johnstons had asked her to come to Dreamflight in the first place. But since she'd arrived, the colt had gotten worse instead of better. Was the Johnstons' new exercise program the problem, or was it her? And then there was Star. What had happened to him since the Louisiana Derby? Had he lost his will to run? Or was she doing something wrong with him, too?

Patrick asked Christina to breeze Callie a half mile alongside Something Wicked, one of Dreamflight's other stakes horses. The dark brown filly had recently won the Santa Anita Oaks, so Christina knew she was fast. Still, the Johnstons made it clear that they expected Callie to beat her. And they wanted the colt to do it by coming from behind in the final quarter mile.

Owen Jordans, the leading jockey of the meet, was riding the filly for the breeze. Owen was only one of several famous riders Christina had met that morning. Aaron had been right when he said that the Johnstons had plenty of jockeys to choose from. So why had they decided to let her ride Callie?

109

Don't worry about that. Concentrate on riding, Christina told herself. *Show them they did the right thing.* But her hands were shaking as she cantered Callie over to the rail alongside Something Wicked.

Callie had been jittery since the moment he stepped onto the track. It was taking all Christina's energy just to keep him straight. Already patches of sweat darkened his bay coat.

"Ready?" Owen called to Christina as they neared the half-mile pole.

"Let's go!" Christina replied, hoping she sounded more confident than she felt.

Something Wicked rushed forward, and Callie jerked his head, trying to chase after the filly. Christina held him back, knowing the Johnstons expected her to wait. Callie tried pulling the reins from her hands, and when that failed, he began darting from side to side, nearly ramming her leg into the rail.

"Easy, Callie," Christina soothed, hoping the colt was listening to her. "Just wait a bit longer. I have to hold you until the three-quarters pole."

Callie didn't change his stride. He continued running like a rocking horse with a broken spring. Christina had to grab his mane to keep her balance.

Something Wicked had taken the lead by over a length and was pulling away. Callie was so busy fighting Christina that he didn't even seem to notice. And when Christina let him go after a quarter mile, he was too tired to respond. He stretched forward and lengthened his stride, but Christina could feel him laboring.

"You can do it, Callie!" she yelled. She kneaded her hands along his neck and even resorted to the whip. Still, Something Wicked increased the gap between them.

Christina had to push Callie through every stride toward the end of the breeze. They finished well behind the other horse.

Immediately Christina stood in her stirrups to slow Callie down. The colt was a mess. His coat was lathered in sweat, and he was breathing hard. Christina patted Callie on his shoulder. "I'm sorry, boy," she whispered. "I know you were trying out there. You just don't like being rated, do you?"

Christina looked up the track. Amanda and Patrick were deep in conversation, unhappy frowns creasing their faces. She was pretty sure she didn't want to know what they were saying, but she had to give them some sort of explanation for the work. Reluctantly she rode Callie back toward the trainers.

"I thought you were following our schedule," Amanda said angrily as Christina approached.

"I have been," Christina replied softly. "I gave him the workouts you wanted, and Deborah seemed to think things were going all right."

"Then how do you explain his time? He hasn't been this slow since he was a yearling! Something Wicked led by over two lengths, and it was a short breeze." Amanda's tone made Christina want to disappear.

"Maybe he was just nervous," Patrick reasoned. He put a hand on his wife's arm. "Does he usually resist you this much, Christina?"

Christina shook her head. "He hates being rated, but I've never seen him this nervous, not even before the Lafayette."

"So maybe this was an off day," Patrick repeated. "I'll tell you what, Christina. I want you to work him again tomorrow, and I expect to see a major improvement."

"Of course," Christina said immediately. "I'll try—"

"If he doesn't run well tomorrow, then we'll put another rider on him for the San Felipe Stakes," Amanda interrupted. "Is that understood?"

Christina nodded, unable to meet the trainer's piercing blue eyes. Fortunately, she saw Aaron leading Star onto the track, and walked Callie over to exchange horses.

"He'll need a good cooling out," Christina said. Her voice was barely a whisper as she tried to contain her emotions. The Johnstons had threatened to replace her, and after what had happened, she could hardly blame them. Christina closed her eyes and pressed her fingers against them, trying to stop the tears. She had to get Callie's horrible breeze out of her mind so she could work Star.

Aaron started to say something, but the look on Christina's white face stopped him. Wordlessly he held Callie's head so Christina could dismount, then handed her Star's reins.

"Thanks," Christina said, trying unsuccessfully to smile. She bit her lower lip, knowing she had to pull herself together.

"You're welcome. Good luck out there," Aaron said, and boosted her into the saddle.

Christina choked back her tears as she sank into Star's saddle. She leaned down to pet her horse, enjoying the feel of his soft coat against her fingers. Aaron put a reassuring hand on her knee for a moment before leading Callie off the track.

"Come on, Star, let's go," Christina whispered half-heartedly. She moved her horse to the outside rail to trot. She was not looking forward to this. Star hadn't put in any brilliant workouts since she had arrived in California. Why would he start now?

Star tossed his head playfully as they jogged down the backside. Normally Christina wouldn't have minded his antics, but this day she jerked back on the reins until he settled down. She had to show everyone at Santa Anita that she could keep her colt's attention.

Christina had asked Deborah to clock Star for a short breeze, only two furlongs. She hoped the shorter distance would give him less time to slack off.

As they neared the starting point for the breeze, Christina considered calling off the work. She knew that she was upset, and she didn't want to make a fool of herself in front of the Johnstons twice. But the Santa Anita Derby was too close for her to give Star another day off.

Before she could change her mind, Christina looked ahead to where Deborah stood on the rail with her stopwatch. As she passed the assistant trainer, Christina asked Star to run.

Star didn't respond. He lumbered forward, barely increasing his pace.

"Come on, Star! Let's run!" Christina kneaded her hands along Star's neck. When this didn't elicit a response, she used the whip.

Star came to a sliding halt. Caught by surprise, Christina barely managed to keep her seat. She lost one of her stirrups and clung to Star's back by grabbing a hank of his copper mane. The colt spun around, almost diving toward the rail, and threw Christina over his side. The handful of mane slipped through her fingers.

Everything seemed to move in slow motion as she

slid out of the saddle. She was almost hyperaware of the sounds around her as she tumbled toward the dirt. There was the pounding of hooves. Star was snorting.

Then the ground rushed up to meet her. Christina landed on her side. For a moment she felt she was going to pass out. The world grew dimmer, the light ebbing until she could hardly see.

"Christina! Christina! Can you hear me?" Deborah's voice seemed so distant.

Christina clutched a handful of dirt until her vision cleared. "I'm all right," she managed to croak. She sat up, ignoring the pain in her back.

"You sure? That was a pretty bad fall."

"Yeah, I'm fine." Christina stood. Her knees wobbled. Deborah held her arm, supporting her. "I'll just get back on and finish." She pulled away from Deborah's grasp and, by sheer force of will, walked up the track. Aaron had caught Star and was walking him in small circles on the outside.

"Are you okay, Christina?" he asked, frowning worriedly.

Christina ignored the question, unsure whether her voice was working. She tried to vault onto Star's saddle but didn't have the strength. Aaron had to give her a leg up and push her trembling legs into the stirrups.

Shakily Christina aimed Star closer to the rail. Still numb with shock, she cantered Star for a furlong, checking for lameness. Fortunately, the colt didn't seem to be hurt.

Christina let Star canter without doing much steering until they reached the far turn. Taking a deep breath, she let Star have his head.

This time Star behaved. He galloped through the next furlong evenly, eating the ground with his strides. The pace was far from magnificent, but Christina didn't have the energy to correct him. Each time Star's hooves hit the ground, twinges of pain shot down her left side. She gritted her teeth, forcing herself through the breeze.

As they entered the second furlong, Star again began to drop the pace. Since she was hardly able to see the track through her tears, Christina pulled back on Star's reins, ending the workout there. Without stopping to talk with anyone from Dreamflight, Christina mechanically went through the motions of cooling Star out and unsaddling him. She felt as if she were moving underwater, yet her thoughts were racing.

Back in his stall, she groomed Star slowly, her hands shaking. She dropped the currycomb into the bedding, and her fingers fumbled as she tried to pick it up. Frustrated, she threw the comb against the back wall of the stall. The noise startled Star, causing him to move away from her.

Christina sank down into the far corner of Star's

stall. She felt tears leak out of the corners of her eyes, and she no longer had the strength to stop them.

"I've messed up everything," Christina choked out. At the sound of her voice, Star walked over and nudged her with his nose. "I came to California thinking that I could solve all our problems, Star. I thought everything would work out if I could just get us away from all the pressure in Kentucky. But the pressure wasn't keeping you from running well. Nothing's changed since we got here. I never should have come."

Christina put one hand to her mouth to muffle the sound of her sobs. With her free hand, she reached up to rub Star's forehead.

"I'm sorry, boy," Christina whispered over and over again. "I never should have brought you here. I'm so, so sorry."

9

CHRISTINA LOST TRACK OF TIME AS SHE CRIED INSIDE STAR'S stall. Every one of her nightmares was coming true. Within the next few days Callie would get a new jockey and Star would lose the Santa Anita Derby. Her dreams of the Triple Crown would come to a crashing halt. More than anything, though, Christina regretted letting Star down.

The sound of someone coming into Star's stall made Christina shrink farther into the corner. She squeezed her eyes shut and pressed her palms against them.

"Shh, Christina. It's going to be all right."

The voice was gentle and soothing. It was Aaron. Dimly she heard the rustle of bedding as Aaron sat down beside her and put an arm around her shaking shoulders. "It's okay. We'll figure something out."

118

Christina took several deep, shuddering breaths in an attempt to compose herself. She didn't want Aaron to see her like this. "I'll be okay," she managed to say. "I just need to be alone."

Aaron didn't move. He tightened his arm around her, holding her as she cried her heart out. Without thinking about what she was doing, Christina leaned against him, letting him support her until the sobs ran their course.

When she finally regained control, Christina pulled away from Aaron, embarrassed. She wiped her face with the back of her hand. "I'm sorry," she croaked.

Aaron stood up and held out his hand. "Come on. We're getting you away from the track."

Christina looked at him through swollen, tear-filled eyes. "Where else can I go?"

"Anywhere but here." Aaron took Christina's hand and pulled her up. "I'm going to take you on that tour of L.A. I promised you."

"But I have to think. I need to find a way to make Star run again," Christina said hoarsely. "I'm running out of time."

"You're in no shape to make any decisions right now," Aaron reasoned. He opened the stall door. "You need to take a break."

Christina shook her head but did not struggle as Aaron led her out of the barn.

Fifteen minutes later Christina had changed out of her riding clothes and was sitting in the passenger seat of Aaron's silver Volkswagen Beetle. She pressed her forehead against the sun-warmed window, watching the road stretch out in front of her.

"So where do you want to go?" Aaron asked.

Christina shrugged. "Any recommendations?" She tried to look excited for Aaron's sake. She was grateful for the other rider's attention. Despite her protests, she really didn't want to be alone.

"Well, Disneyland opened up a new theme park last year. It's called California Adventure. It's very cheesy, but some of the rides are pretty good." Aaron looked at Christina, hoping for a change in her expression.

"Sounds good," Christina replied. She gave Aaron a shaky smile and shifted in her seat, wincing as her sore muscles protested.

As they drove Aaron sang along with the radio for a few songs, encouraging Christina to join in. When they hit a stretch of slow traffic, Aaron turned to Christina and gently asked, "So, do you want to talk about it?"

Christina sighed. "What is there to talk about?" she wondered aloud. "I've messed up everything."

"But you were just following Amanda and Patrick's instructions with Callie, and you've been listening to your parents about Star. Right?"

Christina shrugged her shoulders. "I did all the breezes my parents wanted me to do with Star. I just didn't tell them how bad his times have been. They didn't want me to come out here in the first place." She shrugged again. "I thought I could fix things on my own. I thought I knew Star well enough to make him want to run."

"And you do know Star," Aaron insisted. "I saw the way he listened to you when you rode him that first day at Dreamflight. When he caught Blue Streak at the end, I thought you two could run that fast forever. And I told you how I saw you two win the Louisiana Derby on TV. I bet no one can make Star run like you can."

"The Louisiana Derby was what started this whole mess," Christina replied. "During his two-year-old season, Star was always a late closer. Then, during the Louisiana Derby, he jumped to the front at the beginning of the race and almost scared me to death. I didn't know if he would have enough left at the finish line, but he did, and we won."

"And what makes that so bad?" Aaron wondered.

"Star hasn't run that well since. I know he'll need to run like that for the Triple Crown, but the more I try to get it back, the more it fades." Christina pounded her knee with her fist in frustration. "I've done something to make him lose his will to win."

"That's impossible. You're the one who made him a champion in the first place," Aaron argued.

Christina shook her head. "I think Star has won races despite my riding, not because of it. In our first race together I had no idea what was going on. Everything was moving so fast. It felt like furlongs were passing by before I could react, and Star was last for a while. The only reason we won that day was because I stayed off Star's back and let him do all the work."

I stayed off Star's back and let him do all the work. Christina gasped as she realized her mistake.

"What's wrong?" Aaron demanded.

Christina couldn't reply as the thoughts sorted themselves out in her mind. She closed her eyes and mentally replayed all Star's great races, remembering how the colt had found it in himself to outrun his competition at the wire. She thought back to the moment in the Louisiana Derby when she had known Star was going to win despite his early speed, when all she had needed to do was hang on and let him take her to the finish. He had run like the wind.

She and Star had always made the most of each other's strengths and made up for each other's weaknesses. Over the past few weeks she had been determined to change what was Star's greatest strength—his ability to lengthen his stride down the stretch whenever he needed to.

Of course Star hasn't been running well, Christina thought. *How could he when I haven't been listening to him? First all I could think about was the competition at Keeneland. Then I got so fixated on changing Star's running style and keeping him in the lead the whole time, I forgot to pay attention to* him. *Mom and Dad were right—Star is a closer. He doesn't need a new strategy. He needs me to stay with him throughout a workout so that he's in a position to accelerate when it really matters.*

"Christina? Say something," Aaron said, glancing at her worriedly.

Christina grinned at Aaron. "I know what's been going wrong with Star!" she exclaimed. She had to restrain herself from jumping out of her seat and hugging him in her excitement. She spoke rapidly as she continued, the words tumbling over themselves. "You were right when you praised Star for catching up with Blue Streak at the wire. What he did that day was great. I just couldn't see it because I was so mad at him for the slow start. I thought that if I made him go faster earlier in his breeze, then he wouldn't have time to tease the other horses. But I was concentrating on the wrong thing. Star has always been a closer. All I have to do is keep him focused and put him in a good spot to catch up with the leaders down the stretch. I need to let him do what he does best."

Aaron considered Christina's words. "That sounds

about right," he said. "And maybe that could apply to Callie, too."

Again Christina couldn't believe she had been so unperceptive. Of course what she said applied to Callie!

She had followed the Johnstons' instructions and watched Callie's downward spiral without thinking of ways to correct it. But the Johnstons were wrong about Callie—his early speed didn't have to be a disadvantage. If he put enough distance between himself and his nearest opponent, then he might be able to hold on at the wire. It was certainly a better idea than letting him waste all his energy at the start.

Christina sighed. "You're right, Aaron," she said. "I just wish I had realized all this sooner. Now Star's not going to trust me enough to run well in the Santa Anita Derby, and the Johnstons are going to find another rider for Callie."

"Not if we change their minds tomorrow," Aaron pointed out. "Maybe the horses are just as frustrated as you are. They might be so happy when you let them do what they do best that they'll forget the past week."

"But what if they don't understand what I'm trying to do?" Christina asked. "I wish I could work with them before anyone sees me ride them on the track tomorrow morning."

Aaron was silent for a moment. He drummed his fingers on the steering wheel as he thought. Then he turned to Christina with a mischievous smile. "Maybe you can," he said. "The Johnstons and Deborah are going out to dinner tonight with Callie's owner, Marisa Pavlik. Dinner with her takes hours—I doubt they'll be back at the track tonight."

Christian looked at Aaron questioningly, wondering what he was up to.

"They open up Santa Anita in the evenings for extra training sessions, although few people take advantage of that because of the heat," Aaron continued. "We could take Callie and Star out tonight. There won't be any crowds."

"What happens if the Johnstons find out?" Christina wondered worriedly. She could do whatever she wanted with Star, since he was her horse, but she needed the Johnstons' permission to gallop Callie. How was she going to ask them, though? She couldn't tell them she thought their training strategy was incorrect; if she did, they'd find another rider for Callie without even giving her a chance to prove it.

"Like I said, they'll be at dinner," Aaron replied. "Trust me, Christina, all Patrick and Amanda really care about is the result. They'll be thrilled if you solve Callie's problems."

"And they already want to fire me, so I guess things can't get worse." Christina was warming up to the idea. For the first time in days, she felt she was going to do the right thing.

"They're not going to fire you if you make Callie run faster than he ever has," Aaron assured her. "And I have a feeling Star's going to surprise you out there, too. So, are you in?"

This time Christina didn't hesitate. "Yes," she said. "Let's go for it."

Star snorted uneasily as Christina rode him onto the deserted Santa Anita track. Beside her, Aaron was concentrating on keeping Callie from bucking.

"I think both of them remember this morning," Christina murmured nervously.

The afternoon at California Adventure had been fun. Christina and Aaron had gotten soaked on the water ride, watched 3-D movies, and ridden the Ferris wheel that overlooked the entire park. At the end of the day Aaron had forced Christina to ride the roller coaster with an upside-down loop. "You're a jockey and you used to ride cross-country. No roller coaster can be scary after that," he insisted.

Christina had screamed through the entire ride. Aaron had bought a freeze-frame picture, wanting to preserve her expression as they headed down one of the bigger drops. Despite her protests, he had taped the photo to Star's stall.

But Christina had been unable to completely relax all afternoon. The only thing on her mind had been how she would regain Star's trust.

"Don't worry, Christina. I can control Callie," Aaron said reassuringly as they headed up the track.

"I know you can," Christina said. "I just keep waiting for someone to walk up and kick us off the track." She paused and then added honestly, "And I don't know if I'm up to this." She couldn't forget how abruptly Star had tuned her out that morning. What if he did the same thing again?

"Just take it moment by moment," Aaron replied, still sounding calm. "We'll keep them at a steady canter until the far turn, then try a half-mile breeze."

Christina nodded, taking a deep breath. She could tell already that Star wasn't connecting with her. The colt barely listened to her signal as she asked for a canter, and he responded without any enthusiasm.

"Please, Star," Christina said. She leaned down on Star's neck. "Let's start over."

The colt tossed his head and pinned his ears, and Christina's heart sank. Star wasn't going to listen. She had lost him.

"Ready to run?" Aaron called over. Christina could

127

see Callie fidgeting and foaming at the bit, and she blamed herself again for ruining the other horse.

"Yeah," Christina replied uncertainly.

"Okay, on three." Aaron straightened Callie's zigzagging path in preparation. "One . . . two . . . three!"

Christina gave Star rein. But the colt didn't move forward. Just as he had that morning, he galloped unevenly for a couple of strides before tossing his head and coming to a stop.

This time Christina was ready. She managed to stay on as Star tried to whirl toward the rail.

"It's okay, Star," she said, desperately talking to the colt. Was it too late to make a connection? "I was wrong to do what I did. I forgot all the amazing things you've done. But I'm willing to listen to you now."

Christina ran her hands down Star's neck, trying to get his attention. "No matter how you come out of the gate in May, whether you dash out to the front like you did in Louisiana or you decide to hang back, I know we can still win. As long as we work together, we will always have a chance."

Star moved sideways down the track as she spoke. Christina asked him to canter once more, using her legs to keep him straight, but careful to keep her signals gentle. The colt's ears flicked back and forth as he alternately listened to her and regarded the floodlit track.

"I love you, Star," Christina continued. She'd forgotten about catching up to Callie and was completely focused on her horse. "Just give me one more chance, and I'll make it up to you. I promise."

Star flicked his ears back again and stopped fidgeting. He thrust his nose out, catching sight of Callie way ahead on the track.

"Yes, boy. That's it!" Excitement crept into Christina's voice. "Let's run!"

Star grabbed the bit and lengthened his stride.

"Good boy, Star!" Christina encouraged. She didn't move a muscle, not wanting to interfere with his fluid motion. She had forgotten her goggles, and Star's mane stung her eyes as he ran. But she hardly noticed. Star was back!

Star clicked into high gear, shortening the distance between himself and Callie with every stride.

"Let's get them!" Christina called. "I know you can!"

Star responded to her voice, pouring out even more speed. He wasn't just racing Callie now. He was running against the wind—and winning!

Star cut into Callie's lead until Christina could see the horse's flank to her left. There wasn't much time—the end of the stretch was approaching.

Christina stopped looking at Callie and set her gaze just beyond the imaginary finish line.

Beneath her, Star stretched himself out and ran faster than she'd felt him run in weeks. As they passed the quarter pole they drew even with Aaron and Callie, finishing head-to-head. Christina stood in her stirrups and punched the air triumphantly.

"We did it, Star!" she cried. When Star's pace slowed, she leaned down and wrapped her arms around her colt's neck.

"I think that was a photo finish," Aaron told her as he trotted past them.

"We'll just call it a tie," Christina agreed. She couldn't stop smiling. "How did Callie do?"

"He seemed a bit surprised when I gave him his head, but I managed to convince him everything was all right." Aaron was grinning, too. His brown eyes sparkled beneath the Santa Anita lights. "Callie was going faster than I've ever felt him run, so Star's time when he caught up must have been incredible. Too bad we didn't bring a stopwatch."

"I don't care about his time," Christina said. She hugged her horse again. "Star forgave me. That's what really counts."

10

Spectators were crowded on the rail when the Johnstons asked Christina to ride Callie Wednesday morning. The bay colt reacted to the atmosphere with characteristic nervousness, stamping and snorting. Christina tried hard to listen as Amanda lectured her about how to ride Callie, but it was all she could do to keep the colt from bolting. And she knew that she wasn't going to follow Amanda's orders anyway.

"This is his biggest work before Friday's race," Amanda told her. "Let's try to do what I wanted yesterday. Hold him back for the first quarter and then let him go for the half mile. He'd better look sharp. If he comes out of it like he did yesterday, then we're getting someone else to ride him. His owner flew from

Phoenix to see this workout and the race. I'm not going to disappoint her."

Christina glanced along the rail and guessed that the well-dressed older woman wearing expensive-looking sunglasses was Callie's owner.

"Don't let Amanda get to you," Aaron whispered. He took Callie's reins and led the horse in a tight circle. "If he runs like he did last night, she'll be begging you to ride him."

"I hope so," Christina said. Butterflies fluttered in her stomach. "But what if she gets mad at me for not following her instructions?"

"It's going to be okay," Aaron assured her. "When she sees how much better he goes, there's no way she'll be angry."

Christina nodded, still uncertain. She eased Callie onto the track and began the warm-up. *If I disobey Amanda and Callie doesn't kick in, she's going to replace me for sure,* she thought. *But if I listen to Amanda, I know he won't run, and she'll still replace me. I have nothing to lose,* she reminded herself.

Picking up on her nervousness, Callie began ducking to the outside, jerking his head.

"You're right, Callie. I can't think like that," Christina said gently. Distractions were what had gotten her in trouble in the first place. "I know we'll both look good when you show her what you can do."

Callie skittered toward the rail, ignoring Christina's leg signals. "Easy, boy," she soothed. "We're going to warm up nice and slow and then I'll let you run." She hoped the colt would calm down once she gave him his head.

When Christina cantered Callie past the Johnstons, she saw them shaking their heads. Clearly they didn't expect much from her breeze.

Well, she would show them!

She slid her hands up Callie's neck, asking the colt to run. She grabbed a chunk of his mane, preparing for Callie's rapid acceleration.

But Callie didn't speed up.

A wave of panic washed over Christina. Why wasn't he running? She started to use her crop, then stopped when she remembered Star's reaction. Force wasn't the answer.

"Come on, Callie," she encouraged, kneading her hands against the colt's neck. Her heart raced in panic. Maybe she had been wrong about Callie. His performance the night before could have been a fluke. But even as that thought entered her mind, Christina knew that Callie had been at his best the previous night. She just needed to find a way to get the same response Aaron had gotten.

Thinking of Aaron made Christina remember what he had said about Callie after the breeze. *He seemed a bit surprised when I gave him his head.*

Christina knew why Callie was hesitating. The colt was confused. For the past few days she had been jerking on his mouth every time he tried to go forward. No wonder he wasn't responding.

Leaning down closer to Callie's ears, Christina began talking to the colt. "It's okay, Callie. I'm letting you have your way. Run your heart out! I won't hold you back."

Callie galloped down the track unevenly. Her eyes filled with tears, Christina sank back into the saddle, preparing to walk back to the Johnstons and tell them about her failure.

Feeling Christina relax, Callie leaped forward. The motion nearly unseated Christina. She grabbed the cantle with one hand, pulling herself back into her jockey's crouch. "Attaboy, Callie!" she encouraged. "Let's go!" The colt responded to her voice with another burst of speed.

For the next half mile Callie ran even faster than he had in the Lafayette. The rapid-fire pace of his gallop smoothed out the up-and-down motion of his strides.

Christina didn't need a stopwatch to appreciate how fast Callie was going. The feel of the wind through her ponytail let her know that the performance was incredible.

As they completed the final furlong, Christina concentrated on the rhythm of Callie's strides, searching for any signs that he was getting tired. But the colt's pace didn't drop. They ran past the Dreamflight trainers in one fluid motion, and Callie fought her as she tried to slow him down.

"Wow! Good boy," Christina praised, patting him. She circled Callie a few times and then headed back down the track toward the Johnstons, swallowing nervously. What would they say about her disobeying their orders?

Callie's owner was gesturing animatedly as she spoke to the Johnstons.

"I can't believe that was the same horse we saw yesterday," Patrick said, smiling. "Marisa, meet Christina Reese. She's the one who won the Lafayette with your horse."

Marisa extended a well-manicured hand. Christina took off her glove before shaking it. "Nice to meet you, Ms. Pavlik," Christina said.

"Oh, call me Marisa." The owner gave her colt a few small pats. "I can see that you and my boy get along well."

"I hope so." Christina looked at Amanda, wondering what the trainer was thinking.

"Well, the breeze certainly wasn't what I had in mind," Amanda began. "What happened at the beginning?"

"Callie hates being restrained," Christina said

quickly. "Every time I hold him back, he starts fretting and burns up all his energy. It was getting to the point where he was afraid to run. I wanted to try giving him his head from the beginning to see if that would help, but he didn't trust me until I relaxed completely."

"So you disregarded our instructions on purpose," Amanda said sharply.

Christina shrank back into the saddle. "I'm sorry. I just wanted to calm Callie down and get him to run his best."

"Are you saying that this young lady did something wrong?" Marisa interrupted. "The horse looked wonderful to me."

"But we were trying to retrain him so he could run longer distances," Amanda explained.

"I think he can," Christina said desperately. She no longer cared whether she was Callie's jockey. She just wanted the trainers to believe her so that they wouldn't make Callie miserable. "He has the endurance and stamina to be a distance runner. But if you restrain him, he loses all that and puts everything he has into fighting his rider. I think he has to stay in front from the beginning if you want him to win a distance race."

Patrick looked at Christina critically. "Like Amanda said, this wasn't what we had in mind. But his time speaks for itself. He broke his personal record for a half-mile breeze."

"Does this mean that Christina will be riding Callie in his race on Friday?" Marisa asked.

Christina glanced at the trainers for confirmation. She crossed her fingers.

"Of course she will," Patrick said. Beside him, Amanda eyed Christina for several moments before nodding tightly.

Christina smiled. "Thanks so much," she told the trainers. She then looked over their heads at Aaron, who stood on the rail holding Star. He gave her a thumbs-up.

"We should be thanking you," Patrick corrected. "Now you'd better go work that big bundle of energy of yours—he looks ready to pop."

Christina chuckled. "I think I'm just going to take it easy with him today," she said. After the previous day's amazing run, she didn't want to stress her horse out. "We'll be doing a six-furlong breeze tomorrow."

"Are you sure about that?" Patrick asked. "I heard there were some fireworks during your workout yesterday."

"Yeah, but things are under control now," Christina replied. She didn't look at Aaron, afraid that she would be unable to keep a straight face if she did. The thought of Aaron gave her an idea. "Actually, if you don't mind, I wanted Aaron to ride him so I can see from the ground how he's doing."

Patrick looked at her as though she were crazy. "I don't understand why you're not breezing him today. But Aaron's welcome to ride him if he wants to."

Christina looked at Aaron expectantly. The exercise rider was still recovering from the surprise.

"I-I'd love to ride him," Aaron stammered.

"Let's go, then," Christina said. She took Star's reins from him and led her horse several yards away so that the Johnstons couldn't hear their conversation.

"Look, Christina, I know you told me I could ride Star, but I'll understand if you don't want me to try him so close to race time," Aaron said.

"No, I want you to ride," Christina insisted. "The Johnstons haven't let you exercise any of their horses since you got here, and I know that must be driving you crazy. You helped me solve my problems, so this is the least I can do." She gestured to Star, who was stamping and swishing his tail. "Now get on, and let's put some of his energy to good use." She held the right stirrup while Aaron climbed onto the saddle. "Like I told Patrick, I'm not doing anything fancy this morning. Just a nice slow gallop. He'll probably try to push you into giving him more rein, but he doesn't pull as hard as Callie can."

Aaron nodded. "Just don't laugh when I make a fool of myself."

"Now who needs a confidence boost?" Christina

teased. She leaned against the rail and watched as Aaron worked her colt. Aaron rode Star expertly, keeping the colt in check as his impossibly long strides ate up the track.

As Aaron and Star cantered past the Johnstons on the rail, Christina smiled when she saw the huge grin on the other rider's face. Obviously he was enjoying Star's liquid-smooth gallop. Christina didn't think Aaron had ever looked more handsome.

On the rail, Patrick and Amanda looked on skeptically. She didn't let their assessment bother her. Star had shown his stuff the night before. He was ready for the Santa Anita Derby. She didn't need to push him.

Christina whistled cheerfully as she entered the jockeys' lounge on the day of the San Felipe Stakes. Finally everything was falling into place for both Star and Callie. The previous day she had drilled Star through six furlongs. Though Star had taken the first couple slowly, he had sped up so much during the last quarter mile that his time had been the fastest recorded that day.

Although Christina had given Star just a light workout that morning in preparation for the next day's race, the colt had been in high spirits and had anticipated her commands, obeying her instantly. She wished someone at Whitebrook could see them now.

Both she and Star were so much happier than they had been at Keeneland.

As she changed into Dreamflight's green-and-white diamond-patterned silks, Christina stopped whistling. Despite all the tension that she had faced at Keeneland, she found herself missing the company of familiar faces at the track. It was lonely here in the Santa Anita jockeys' dressing room.

Well, I'll be home soon—with two more wins behind me, I hope.

After she changed, Christina wove through the groups of jockeys playing pool in the lounge and settled on one of the couches to watch the races on the television monitors. From the other jockeys' conversation, Christina figured out that the track was fast along the rail but deep on the outside. She had drawn the number seven position. She would have to get Callie to the rail quickly to keep him on the good surface.

Feeling the first twinges of nervousness, Christina closed her eyes and thought about the silly movie Aaron had taken her to see the night before. Jessica and Anisa had met them at the movie theater, and she had heard them teasing Aaron about her when they thought she couldn't hear.

Christina allowed herself to admit that she was definitely starting to like Aaron. He was the most relaxed and sympathetic boy she had ever met, and he had a silly side that revealed itself off the track. But Christina knew that she couldn't get into any sort of relationship just then, not with the Triple Crown coming up. Besides, she was leaving California on Monday and might never see Aaron again.

Christina laughed at her own thoughts. Her friends often teased her that she didn't talk about anything that didn't have four legs. She wondered what they would say if they could hear her thoughts now.

The announcement of post time broke Christina out of her musings. She lined up with all the other jockeys and looked out onto the Santa Anita track as they walked to the gate. This track still seemed strange compared to the Kentucky racecourses. And the sun beat down, hotter and brighter than ever.

Patrick and Amanda were fussing over Callie in the walking ring. Aaron was holding the colt's head, trying to keep him from moving backward.

"You look great in those silks," Aaron whispered to her as she passed. "Save some room for me in the winner's circle picture, okay?"

"Of course," Christina replied. She turned to Patrick. "So I hear Truth and Rumors is the horse to beat," she said.

Patrick nodded. He pointed to the black horse. "He's a late closer, so you'll really have to watch out at the wire."

"Any other closers in this race?" Christina asked.

"Eat My Dust will definitely be a factor. He's won a bunch of races on the northern California tracks," Amanda said.

"With a little luck, Callie will have such a big lead coming down the stretch that we won't have to worry about any of them, right?" Christina said, trying to sound confident.

"Yeah. It's a risk not rating him in such a long race, though. He'll have to go wire to wire over a mile and a sixteenth," Amanda pointed out.

"But we know he can do it," Patrick told Christina confidently as the escort rider appeared to lead Callie to the track. "Good luck."

11

"AND THE HORSES ARE LOADING FOR THE SAN FELIPE Stakes." The announcer's voice carried through the infield to the track, where Christina was circling Callie, waiting to enter the starting gate. She was glad they would be among the last to load.

Just as the attendants called her number, one of the other horses reared, startling Callie. The bay colt backed away from the gate.

"Easy, boy. Easy," Christina soothed. "Let's just get in there and run our race, okay?" To her relief, the colt obeyed, loading smoothly.

"We're going wire to wire, Callie," Christina whispered as the final horse loaded and she prepared for the lurching start.

For a moment silence swept through the crowds. Then the gates crashed open.

They were off!

Callie broke sharply and edged to the rail. Christina steered him through the crush of horses, careful not to interfere with any of them.

"And Calm Before the Storm jumps to an early lead." Christina barely made out the announcer's voice over the sound of pounding hooves. Callie pushed forward on his own, lengthening his stride as they streaked through the first turn. Christina angled him close to the rail to save ground. She focused on the rhythm of Callie's churning strides and encouraged the colt to keep running.

"Forty-four seconds for the half! That's almost record time!" the announcer screamed. "Calm Before the Storm has a three-length lead!"

Christina let herself glance back. Callie's pace had left most of the field behind, but the closers were only beginning their run. Would Callie have enough left to maintain his lead?

Callie continued running strongly through the next quarter mile. But Christina could tell the colt was reaching his limit. He was no longer stretching his head as far when his front legs hit the ground. She looked back again. Several horses were definitely gaining on them.

"Calm Before the Storm still leads by two lengths as they round the far turn! He ran the six furlongs in a minute and seven seconds! But Truth and Rumors is gaining on the outside. He's followed by Eat My Dust and Mandolin on the rail. . . ."

"Come on, Callie!" Christina yelled. "I know you have something left." She asked the horse to change leads, hoping that would give him an extra surge of speed. There was less than a quarter mile to go.

Knowing that Callie was giving all that he had, Christina didn't use her whip down the stretch. She pushed her hands along the colt's neck and kept talking as Callie drew on the last of his reserves.

The other horses were getting closer. One was trying to squeeze between Callie and the rail, while the other was coming up on the outside. Callie flicked his tail in distress as one horse drew even with his flank.

Christina could see the wire just ahead of them. Her only hope was that it would come soon. Callie's pace was dropping quickly. She could see Truth and Rumors's head out of the corner of her eye.

But Callie refused to be defeated. Christina felt him tense his hindquarters and push off one last time. They were under the wire!

"And Calm Before the Storm manages an incredible wire-to-wire victory, holding off the favorite, Truth and Rumors, by a head! What a courageous performance by the Dreamflight colt!"

"Do you hear that, Callie? They're talking about you." Christina stood in her stirrups to halt Callie's ragged gallop. The colt broke into an uneven trot and then came to a stop almost immediately. Christina looked at the horse with concern. Callie's coat was black with sweat, and his sides heaved as he took huge breaths.

"You gave it everything you had, didn't you?" Christina asked, running her hands down his neck. The colt, still wired from the race, tossed his head.

An escort rider met her on the track. "Wow! That was an amazing effort," he praised. "No one can believe that a sprinter beat all these horses at a mile and a sixteenth. You rode him perfectly."

"Thanks," Christina said. She couldn't stop smiling. She had won one of the races she had come to California for. She hoped she wouldn't be pushing her luck to ask for another win the next day with Star.

"I'd like to propose a toast," Patrick said later that night. The Johnstons had insisted on taking Christina out to FrontRunner, the gourmet restaurant at the track. "To Christina and Callie."

146

Amanda and Deborah raised their wineglasses to her.

"It's too bad Callie can't be here. He did all the work," Christina said modestly. She sipped her soda. After the race, she and Aaron had lavished attention on the exhausted horse. When Christina had left to change for dinner, Aaron had been massaging Callie's legs and shoulders, stopping only to feed him another carrot.

Deborah laughed. "I doubt he'd appreciate a glass of champagne," she joked.

"So do you think he's Kentucky Derby material?" Amanda asked Christina. "After today, we're pretty encouraged."

Christina knew what the trainers wanted to hear, but the image of how exhausted Callie had been after running a mile and a sixteenth stuck in her mind. Asking the colt to run a mile and a quarter would be too much. Despite his win that day, Callie still ran like a sprinter. If Callie were her horse, the only Triple Crown race she would consider for him was the Preakness, the shortest of the three.

"Christina? What do you think?" Patrick asked.

Deciding to be honest, Christina took a deep breath. She exhaled slowly as she spoke. "We got lucky today," she admitted. "If the race had been even a few

147

yards longer, then Callie wouldn't have held on."

"But he showed today that he can go the distance. I want to make sure we work him up to his full potential," Amanda argued.

"You might have better luck if you skipped the Derby and went straight to the Preakness," Christina suggested, hoping she wouldn't upset the trainers. The more she thought about the idea, the better it sounded for Callie. "You could give him some time to rest after this and spend some extra time conditioning him for the distance."

"That's not a bad idea," Patrick replied. "We would have a fresh horse going into the Preakness and maybe take some of the others by surprise." He smiled at Christina. "It's too bad you're committed to riding your colt for the Triple Crown. We're going to have a hard time replacing you."

As Christina tried to think of another jockey who could ride the high-strung colt, she remembered the secret night workout, when Aaron had managed to make Callie run again. "I think Aaron would be a good rider for him," she said. The words tumbled out before she could consider how the trainers would react to them.

"Aaron doesn't even have a license yet," Amanda said dismissively.

"He could get one," Christina said. She didn't want to make the trainers angry, but she really felt Aaron deserved the chance. "I've seen him riding all the two-year-olds, and he handles them perfectly. I think he would be able to keep Callie calm before a race."

"It's certainly something to think about," Deborah agreed. "He's been doing a great job with all the horses at the farm."

Amanda nodded. "We'll talk about that later. Tonight, let's celebrate." She put down her fork and looked at Christina. "Do you have any plans for the summer, Christina?" she asked.

"Well, I'll probably be riding Star and some other Whitebrook horses," Christina answered.

"Well, if you decide to give Star a break after the Triple Crown, Patrick and I would like you to come back to Dreamflight," Amanda offered. "We could give you a position as one of our regular jockeys, and you could fly out to Saratoga with us."

Christina had to keep her mouth from dropping open. An opportunity like this would help her establish herself as a professional, separate from her parents. But despite how thrilling the offer sounded, Christina knew she couldn't accept it just yet. Star was still her first priority, and she had the other horses at Whitebrook to think about as well.

"You don't have to let us know right away," Patrick said, seeing Christina's expression. "Just keep it in mind."

"I will," Christina assured him. "Thanks so much for considering me."

The rest of the meal passed in a blur. Christina played with her food as she thought about the Santa Anita Derby the following day. After finishing her dessert, Christina decided to visit Star and Callie before returning to the motel. She stopped by Star's stall first, hoping the sight of her horse would calm her worries about the next day's race. Star recognized her footsteps and stuck his head over the stall door as she approached.

Christina let herself into his stall and hugged her horse, not caring when he rubbed his nose against her dark blue sundress. "Are you ready to race tomorrow, boy?"

Star bobbed his head.

"I know you are. We're going to show these West Coast people what Whitebrook horses can do, right?" Christina pressed her cheek against Star's face, relaxing as the colt lipped her hair.

Out of the corner of her eye, Christina saw Aaron coming toward them, and she reluctantly straightened up.

"I wish I had my camera," Aaron said as he reached

up to pet Star. "You're probably the only person in the world who would go into a stall wearing such a beautiful dress."

Christina shrugged. "I needed to talk with Star about tomorrow."

"Well, I hope he told you not to worry because he was going to annihilate the competition." Aaron offered Star a section of orange.

"Are you sure he'll eat that?" Christina asked skeptically. Star was sniffing the new treat uncertainly.

"Sure. All the Dreamflight horses love them." As if he could understand, Star extended his neck and snapped up the orange. He bit down hard, spraying orange juice everywhere.

Christina laughed and hugged Star again. "How's Callie?" she asked.

"He's sleeping. He wouldn't touch his feed until I mixed in some molasses."

"Well, he deserves to be spoiled after what he did today," Christina replied. "And while you were spoiling him, I worked out a little surprise for you."

Aaron looked confused. "What is that?"

"The Johnstons want to enter Callie in the Preakness. Since I'm committed to riding Star, I suggested that they ask you to ride him."

Aaron's brown eyes widened. "What?" he sputtered.

"I wanted to tell them how you rode him Tuesday night, but I restrained myself," Christina added, enjoying the moment. "Anyway, I figured this gives you enough time to qualify for your license."

"But the Preakness," Aaron protested. "I wasn't planning on racing so soon."

"I know. That's why you would be the perfect jockey for Callie." When Aaron looked confused, Christina added, "Callie needs someone laid back to keep him from stressing out before a race. You're the most relaxed rider I've met." Christina smiled. "Actually, you're probably the only rider I've met who's not too competitive for your own good."

"And that's one of the things I worry about. I don't know if I want to spend my life competing against my friends," Aaron said.

"I think about that all the time, too," Christina said with a sigh. "I mean, one of the reasons I came here was to avoid all the competitiveness back home."

"So how are you going to deal with it when you get back?" Aaron asked.

Christina shrugged. "I still don't know," she admitted. "But when I was sitting in the jockeys' dressing room at Santa Anita today, I realized that I would rather have my friends around and be competing against them than be alone before a race." She let herself out of Star's stall. "I'm probably not the best person to ask about dealing with the tension. What I can tell you, though, is that riding in a race is the best feeling in the world. When I was on the track today, it wasn't so much about beating the other horses as it was about making Callie run his best."

"And you succeeded," Aaron said. "For the record, I think you've dealt with the pre-Derby hype pretty well."

"Well, if we're going on the record, then I'm going to say that you'd better qualify for that jockey's license soon so that my suggestion to the Johnstons doesn't sound completely ridiculous," Christina teased.

"What if I promise to schedule a gate test if you promise to call me when you're back in Kentucky and stuff is getting to you?" Aaron asked.

Christina smiled. "Sounds like I'm getting the better end of that deal," she replied.

"Let's shake on it, then." Aaron extended his hand and Christina shook it. For a long moment neither of them let go.

At last Christina managed to break eye contact, and she pulled her hand away awkwardly.

"I'm sorry," Aaron said quickly.

Christina shook her head. "No, you didn't do anything wrong." She stared at the floor, realizing that she owed Aaron an explanation. "I haven't been completely honest with you," she mumbled.

"About what?"

Wanting to get it over with all at once, Christina said, "I just broke up with my boyfriend of almost two years a few weeks ago." She turned to pet Star so she wouldn't see Aaron's reaction. He remained silent. "I probably should have told you this when we started talking. I just didn't know how." Christina paused. "You've been so great to me since I got to California, Aaron. You're probably my only real friend here."

"You just aren't over your ex-boyfriend yet," Aaron said. His voice was barely audible.

"Right," Christina admitted. "But that's not what I'm really worried about. One of the reasons I broke up with Parker was because I got so busy with Star that I didn't have time for anything else. With the Derby coming up, things are only going to get crazier." She forced herself to look in Aaron's direction. "Still, you're the only person I've been thinking of lately," she said sincerely. "You were there for me when everything fell apart. You kept me from feeling alone. I don't think I'll ever be able to thank you enough for everything you've done since I got here."

"I think giving me a chance to ride in the Preakness is thanks enough," Aaron replied. His glance moved to the picture of the two of them on the roller coaster. He started taking off the tape that held it next to the stall door.

Christina put a hand on the picture. "Please don't be mad, Aaron," she pleaded. "I do care about you. Spending time with you has made me see that there is something beyond the Triple Crown. I haven't had this much fun outside the track in a long time. If I weren't leaving in two days, maybe things could have been different."

"But you are leaving," Aaron pointed out. He continued picking at the tape.

"That doesn't mean we can't keep our deal," Christina said. "I still want to hear all about your gate test and about how Callie's doing. And I want to tell you about Star. You're one of the few people who will understand." Christina covered Aaron's hand with hers, prompting him to look at her. "I'm going to miss you."

Aaron stared at her. She could see the conflicting emotions in his eyes, but she didn't say anything more. She could only hope that she hadn't lost him as a friend.

"I'll miss you, too, Christina," Aaron said. "But I'm going to insist on one more condition to our deal," he added. "I'm sure I'll be seeing you at the track again, possibly at Pimlico. You have to promise me that the next time I see you, you will let me take you out to dinner."

Christina smiled. "That would be great."

12

A KNOCK AT THE DOOR WOKE CHRISTINA FROM A DEEP SLEEP. She looked over at her alarm clock. It was almost seven. "Why didn't Deborah wake me up?" Christina murmured as she walked over to the door, stifling a yawn.

She and Aaron had stayed up late the previous night. They had sat by the fountain, laughing as they exchanged horse stories. The conversation had stopped only when Christina looked down at her watch and realized it was past midnight.

Groggily Christina looked through the peephole. The sight of Ashleigh standing in the doorway woke her instantly. She had almost forgotten her mother's promise to fly down for the Santa Anita Derby.

"I can see you've had a rough morning," Ashleigh teased. She gave her daughter a hug.

"Can't I sleep in every once in a while?" Christina asked defensively.

"Given your great race yesterday, of course you can," Ashleigh said. "I've been reading all about the San Felipe Stakes in the local papers. All the reporters agree that you did an amazing job. I hope you told them I taught you all you know," she added jokingly.

"Of course I did," Christina replied, grinning. "How are things going at Keeneland?"

"We've been doing well," Ashleigh told her. "But let's talk about it later. We need to get you ready for your race today."

Christina began stuffing her silks into a duffel bag. "So how's Star?" Ashleigh asked.

"I haven't worked him hard since he sped through six furlongs the day before yesterday," Christina answered. "I think he's ready for the race. The only thing I'm worried about is that I don't know which Star will show up today. Is he going to do what he did at the Louisiana Derby, or will he run like a closer?"

"I'm sure you'll be ready for whatever happens," Ashleigh assured her.

"I hope so. A few days ago I thought that coming here was going to end in complete disaster," Christina admitted.

"I have to admit I wasn't thrilled by the idea at first," Ashleigh said. "But after hearing Star's time for those six furlongs, I'm pretty sure you did the right thing."

Christina gave her mother another hug to show how much her approval meant to her. "Thanks, Mom," she said.

For the second day in a row Christina stared at the Santa Anita track as she made her way to the walking ring. Her mother and Aaron were waiting with Star.

"Any last-minute advice?" Christina asked, trying to keep the nervous catch from her voice. She looked over at Pocket Money. The light chestnut horse looked to be about eighteen hands tall. He towered above his grooms and trainers as he reared.

Ashleigh shook her head. "You know how to ride him. Just stay focused and don't panic if things get bad early. You have a mile and an eighth to let things play out."

"Yeah, don't forget how Star managed to catch Callie in the final furlong that night," Aaron added. He took Christina's hand and squeezed it.

Christina squeezed back before walking over to Star. "Hey, beautiful," she said, dropping a kiss on his nose. "You know we can do this, right?" Christina looked into Star's soft brown eyes, gaining confidence as she stroked her horse.

"Go get 'em, Christina," Aaron said as he gave her a leg up.

"Good luck," Ashleigh said. "See you in the winner's circle."

For a second after the escort rider led her away, panic consumed Christina. Her stomach churned, her hands shook so much that she couldn't hold the reins, and she couldn't breathe. What on earth had she been thinking? She had dragged her horse to an unfamiliar place to race him against horses she didn't know anything about.

Then Star craned his neck around, trying to nudge her, and the feeling dissipated. "I love you, Star," she whispered. "Keeneland, Santa Anita—it doesn't matter. We're racing together, just like we're supposed to."

So that the nervousness wouldn't control her, Christina kept talking to Star during the post parade. Her bond with the colt seemed stronger now, almost as if she could tell what Star was thinking.

Star entered the gate without protest. He had drawn the number three position, right next to Pocket Money. Christina had watched several tapes of Pocket Money's races. The West Coast star was also a powerful late closer. He had won his last race by seven lengths.

"This is it, Star. Our last race before the Triple Crown," she whispered. "Let's give them all something to talk about."

Christina watched the track intently, anticipating the start. Then the buzzer sounded, and the metal doors snapped open. Star was out like a shot.

Christina crouched low, steadying Star as the colt pushed forward. The break had been clean and fast, and they were among the leaders. Dirt sprayed at Christina from all sides.

Feel his rhythm, Christina told herself. *Don't get upset if he slows*. She looked to her left and, seeing nothing, edged the colt closer to the rail. Star was running easily, fighting for rein but not showing the same early speed he had displayed in Louisiana.

"After the first quarter mile, it's Manifest Destiny in the lead, followed by Tuff Stuff and Instant Replay. Wonder's Star is two lengths behind, and then it's Pocket Money, Kryptonite, and . . ."

Christina could tell that Star wasn't quite ready to extend his stride, so she looked up the track, wanting to position him for a closing strike. Manifest Destiny was dropping back, leaving a gap between horses. Christina readied Star to move into it.

Suddenly Manifest Destiny went down! The jockey flew over the horse's head and landed on the other side of the rail. The other jockeys maneuvered sideways to avoid running into the fallen horse.

Christina hauled on her right rein, trying to move Star to the outside. Her heart was pounding even faster than Star's hooves. The downed horse was directly in their path!

Christina checked Star hard, hoping to slow her horse's momentum. Star shook his head, unable to understand why she wanted him to decrease his pace.

"Please, Star," Christina begged. She kept pulling on the reins. Her days of cross-country jumping enabled her to gauge their distance from the fallen horse. They had only two more strides left until they crashed.

Star caught sight of the fallen horse only one stride away, and Christina felt the colt gather his hindquarters. Then Star leaped sideways, managing to stay clear of Manifest Destiny's thrashing legs.

Christina let out a breath she hadn't realized she had been holding. They had come so close to going down. Beneath her, she could feel Star's legs churning steadily. The rhythm reassured her, reminding her that they were all right. And they still had a race to run.

For several strides Christina checked her colt for lameness. Star wasn't hesitating. In fact, he lowered his head and began powering forward on his own.

Christina looked up the track. The race was more than half over, and Star was among the last horses in the pack.

"Don't panic," Christina told Star, but it was more for her own ears. She was pretty sure they were out of

161

the running, but she owed it to Star to try anyway.

"Let's go!" she cried, pumping her hands down Star's neck. The colt was flying now. He easily passed two fading horses, leaving only five in front of them.

Newly determined, Christina pushed all thoughts of defeat out of her mind. Nothing mattered but her and Star. They were going to show the world what they could do. The wind whistled in her ears and blew her breath away as Star gained on the field. Dirt spattered her goggles when they drew close to the clump of running horses.

"Attaboy, Star!" Christina encouraged. She steered him to the inside, passing three more horses as if they were standing still.

Tears of happiness stung Christina's eyes. She didn't care how they placed that day—her horse had more heart than all the other horses in the field put together.

"Down the stretch they come! Pocket Money holds a three-length lead over Kryptonite. But the real surprise is Wonder's Star! He's moved ahead to third, only four lengths off the leader."

Four lengths. It was too much to make up in one and a half furlongs, but Christina and Star weren't about to give up.

Star was going so fast that his legs no longer seemed to touch the track. Christina was as one with her colt. He responded to her signals almost before she could give them.

With a few more leaping strides, Star passed Kryptonite. "That's it, Star!" Christina cried.

She looked between her horse's ears. They had a clear path to the wire. Pocket Money was still ahead, but they were gaining on him with every stride. Star was giving her everything he had, running for the sheer love of it.

Christina almost laughed out loud in delight. In all her Kentucky Derby fantasies, she had never imagined this—how right it would feel when everything was going well. No matter how Star did in his Triple Crown races, she would be happy as long as they continued to have moments like this on the track.

The finish line flashed by, and Christina heard the roar of the crowd. She looked to her right and saw Owen Jordans, Pocket Money's jockey, waving his crop triumphantly.

"And Pocket Money wins the Santa Anita Derby by half a length!" the announcer cried. "But the horse everyone will be talking about is Wonder's Star. The Kentucky colt was twelve lengths behind, but he ran the last three furlongs of the race in thirty-three seconds! What an effort!"

Christina felt no disappointment. She was so proud of Star that she thought her heart might burst. As she pulled him down to a jog, she checked his condition. His coat was dark with lather, but he wasn't blowing too hard. In fact, he leaned against the bit, as if he wanted to run some more.

Although she knew it was unprofessional, Christina took her feet out of the stirrups so that she could wrap her arms around her horse's neck. "You were incredible, boy! You just kept giving and giving. And you still have more left!" Star whuffed as he heard the sound of her voice. "If we'd had another few yards, you would have left everyone in the dust. And we'll get that extra distance in the Kentucky Derby, boy. We'll get our chance." Christina tightened her grip around her horse's neck. "I love you, Star," she whispered. "You're the best horse in the world."

Christina's mother and Aaron were waiting when the outrider led Christina back to the grandstand. Aaron helped Christina dismount, taking hold of her arm as her legs wobbled beneath her. "You and Star were wonderful out there. That was racing at its finest," he said. He gave her an enthusiastic hug, lifting her off the ground, and then kissed her on the cheek.

"You two scared me for a moment back there. But when he started running again, it took my breath away," Ashleigh said, patting Star. "He certainly inherited his mother's spirit."

"Star ran like a dream, Mom," Christina said, still in a daze. "He was perfect."

A television reporter shoved a microphone in her face. "Christina, after today's race, do you have any regrets about entering Wonder's Star in the Santa Anita Derby rather than the Bluegrass Stakes?"

Ashleigh started to speak to the reporter, but Christina interrupted her. "No, I have no regrets. Star has made amazing progress here in California, and I couldn't be happier with how he ran today."

"So what are your plans for Wonder's Star now?"

Christina grinned. This was one question she was sure about the answer to. She leaned into the microphone and said, "We'll see you at the Kentucky Derby!"

JENNIFER CHU grew up reading every horse book she could get her hands on and has been a fan of the Thoroughbred series since she was twelve years old. She is currently a senior at Stanford University, where she spends most of her free time riding both English and Western for the Stanford Equestrian Team and competing on the Intercollegiate Horse Show Association circuit. This is her first novel for young adults.

WIN!

A TRIP TO A KENTUCKY THOROUGHBRED FARM

ENTER THE Thoroughbred Horse Farm SWEEPSTAKES!

COMPLETE THIS ENTRY FORM • NO PURCHASE NECESSARY.

NAME: _____

ADDRESS: _____

CITY: _____ STATE: _____ ZIP: _____

PHONE: _____ AGE: _____

MAIL TO: THOROUGHBRED HORSE FARM SWEEPSTAKES!
c/o HarperCollins, Attn: Department AW
10 E. 53rd Street   New York, NY 10022

HarperEntertainment

17th Street Productions,
an Alloy Online, Inc., company

THOROUGHBRED 51 CONTEST RULES
OFFICIAL RULES

1. No purchase necessary.

2. To enter, complete the official entry form or hand print your name, address, and phone number along with the words "Thoroughbred Horse Farm Sweepstakes" on a 3"x 5" card and mail to: HarperCollins, Attn.: Department AW, 10 E. 53rd Street, New York, NY 10022. Entries must be received by June 1, 2002. Enter as often as you wish, but each entry must be mailed separately. One entry per envelope. No facsimiles accepted. Partially completed, illegible, or mechanically reproduced entries will not be accepted. Sponsors are not responsible for lost, late, mutilated, illegible, stolen, postage due, incomplete, or misdirected entries. All entries become the property of HarperCollins and will not be returned.

3. Sweepstakes open to all legal residents of the United States (excluding residents of Colorado and Rhode Island), who are between the ages of eight and sixteen by June 1, 2002, excluding employees and immediate family members of HarperCollins, Alloy Online, Inc., or 17th Street Productions, an Alloy Online, Inc., company and their respective subsidiaries, and affiliates, officers, directors, shareholders, employees, agents, attorneys and other representatives (individually and collectively), and their respective parent companies, affiliates, subsidiaries, advertising, promotion and fulfillments agencies, and the persons with whom each of the above are domiciled. Offer void where prohibited or restricted.

4. Odds of winning depend on total number of entries received. Approximately 100,000 entry forms distributed. All prizes will be awarded. Winners will be ran-

drawn on or about June 15, 2002, by representatives of HarperCollins, whose
\.ions are final. Potential winners will be notified by mail and a parent or
\.rdian of the potential winner will be required to sign and return an affadavit of
\.gibility and release of liability within 14 days of notification. Failure to return affadavit within time period will disqualify winner and another winner will be chosen.
By acceptance of prize, winner consents to the use of his or her name, photographs,
likeness, and personal information by HarperCollins, Alloy Online, Inc., and 17th
Street Productions, an Alloy Online, Inc., company for publicity and advertising
purposes without further compensation except where prohibited.

5. One (1) Grand Prize Winner will receive a visit to a Thoroughbred horse farm.
   HarperCollins reserves the right at its sole discretion to substitute another prize of
   equal or of greater value in the event prize is unavailable. All expenses not stated are
   the winner's sole expense.

6. HarperEntertainment will provide the contest winner and one parent or legal
   guardian with round-trip coach air transportation from major airport nearest winner to Lexington, Kentucky, visit to a Thoroughbred horse farm, and standard hotel
   accommodations for a two-night stay. All additional expenses including taxes,
   meals, and incidentals are the responsibility of the prize winner. Approximate retail
   value $2,500.00. Airline, hotel, and other travel arrangements will be made by
   HarperCollins in its discretion. HarperCollins reserves the right to substitute a cash
   payment of $2,500.00 for the Grand Prize. Travel and use of hotel are at risk of win-
   ner and HarperCollins does not assume any liability. All travel arrangements will be
   made by HarperCollins. Trip must be taken by one year from the date prize is
   awarded; certain blackout dates may apply.

7. Only one prize will be awarded per individual, family, or household. Prizes are non-
   transferable and cannot be sold or redeemed for cash. No cash substitute is available
   except at the sole discretion of HarperCollins for reasons of prize unavailability.
   Any federal, state, or local taxes are the responsibility of the winner.

8. Additional terms: By participating, entrants agree a) to the official rules and decisions of the judges which will be final in all respects; and b) to release, discharge, and
   hold harmless HarperCollins, Alloy Online, Inc., and 17th Street Productions, an
   Alloy Online, Inc., company and their affiliates, subsidiaries, and advertising promotion agencies from and against any and all liability or damages associated with
   acceptance, use, or misuse of any prize received in this sweepstakes.

9. To obtain the name of the winners, please send your request and a self-addressed
   stamped envelope (not required for residents of Vermont and Washington) to
   HarperCollins, Attn.: Department AW, 10 E. 53rd Street, New York, NY 10022.